C000212799

Mills & Boon

BEST SELLER ROMANCE

A chance to read and collect some of the best-loved novels from Mills & Boon—the world's largest publisher of romantic fiction.

Every month, four titles by favourite Mills & Boon authors will be re-published in the *Best Seller Romance* series.

A list of other titles in the *Best Seller Romance* series can be found at the end of this book.

Sally Wentworth

RIGHTFUL POSSESSION

MILLS & BOON LIMITED

15–16 BROOK'S MEWS
LONDON W1A 1DR

First published in Great Britain 1978
by Mills & Boon Limited

© Sally Wentworth 1978

Australian copyright 1978
Philippine copyright 1978
This edition 1984

ISBN 0 263 74926 6

Set in Linotype Pilgrim 10 on $11\frac{1}{2}$ pt.
02–1084

Made and Printed in Great Britain by
Richard Clay (The Chaucer Press) Ltd,
Bungay, Suffolk

CHAPTER ONE

'STEWARDESS, I'd like some more coffee.'

'Certainly, madam. Black or white?' Genista Grey turned with a smile that was still warm even after the all-night flight from Hong Kong.

The woman who had addressed her hadn't fared quite so well, though, for despite her thick make-up, the wrinkles round her eyes and the peevish lines of her mouth had started to show. She took the coffee without a word of thanks and Genista pushed the heavy serving trolley back to the galley. Her fellow stewardess, Lyn Marshall, with whom she shared a flat in London, was already there stacking the empty plastic breakfast trays into the rubbish containers to be collected as soon as they landed.

'That's the first class finished,' Genista said rather tiredly. 'Phew, what a night! I doubt if we've been off our feet for longer than five minutes the whole trip. Whoever said that being an air stewardess was a glamour job ought to have tried it today!'

'I'll tell you who said it,' Lyn interjected tartly. 'It was some bald-headed, sex-starved businessman who wanted to be waited on and pandered to by young, good-looking girls instead of his ugly old wife!'

Genista had to laugh, but she sensed the undercurrent of anger in Lyn's voice. 'Having trouble?' she asked sympathetically.

'Oh, no more than the usual occupational hazard, I

suppose. It's that fat, greasy type in seat F3. He's hardly stopped drinking all night and now he's starting to get fresh. Honestly, just who do these men think they are? They're usually middle-aged, balding and fat, and yet they think they only have to make a pass and we'll throw ourselves into their laps and start stripping off there and then!'

'Hey, simmer down!' Genista broke in hurriedly, seeing that her friend was close to either losing her temper or bursting into tears. 'We'll be home by five and then we can go to bed and sleep the clock round. Here, I'll finish stacking those. You go and sit down for a few minutes.'

Lyn dropped gratefully on the seat and kicked off her shoes. 'Ugh, my feet are killing me,' she muttered as she lifted one leg to massage her toes.

'You shouldn't have stayed at that night-club so late yesterday. You could only have had a couple of hours' sleep before check-in time.'

'Mm, I suppose so, but things got pretty hectic after we ran into that Pan-American crowd,' Lyn admitted. 'It was somebody's birthday and they really celebrated in a big way.'

'And I suppose you've been suffering from a hangover ever since. Serves you right!'

'I might have a slight headache,' Lyn answered with dignity, but spoiled the whole effect by adding waspishly, 'And you needn't act so goody-goody either, Gen. The only reason you didn't go along was because you're going out with Paul tonight.' Then she grinned. 'Still, I suppose if I had a date with the best-looking pilot in the whole of Globe Airways I would have probably stayed in myself.'

A buzzer sounded above their heads and Lyn put her head through the curtains to see who wanted attention. The red illuminated call sign over seat F3 glowed brightly in the semi-darkness of the cabin.

'Oh darn! It's lover-boy again,' Lyn said exasperatedly.

'Never mind, I'll go.' Genista walked down the gangway between the double rows of seats and reached to flick off the call button in the console. 'Can I help you, sir?'

The man looked up at her owlishly through his thick glasses. 'I wanted the other stewardess,' he said, slurring his words.

'I'm so sorry, sir, but the second stewardess is busy.'

'You'll do just as well.' His eyes swept over her, mentally undressing her. Genista's own eyes became very cold, but she still held the small, polite smile on her lips. 'I'll have a whisky on the rocks.'

'Very good, sir.' She went back to the galley and collected a glass with ice cubes and a miniature of whisky which she poured out and placed on the man's plastic tray in front of him. He gave her the money for the drink and then deliberately dropped a twenty-pound note on the floor so that she had to stoop to retrieve it. Before she could straighten up he had put an arm round her waist.

'There are plenty more of those where that one came from, beautiful. How about you and me having a really good time tonight?' He leered lasciviously at her, his breath reeking of the whisky he had already drunk.

Genista stood up quickly and gave him an absolutely brilliant smile. 'Are you enjoying your trip, sir?'

He looked slightly taken aback by the question. 'Why, yes. Sure.'

'Then perhaps you would care to go forward to the crew's quarters and tell the Captain how much you're enjoying it? You'll know the Captain quite easily; he's the very hefty man—and he just happens to be my husband! And I'm sure the Second Officer would be pleased to talk to you, too. He's similar in build to the Captain but taller—and he's engaged to the second stewardess.' She stepped to one side to motion him forward. 'If you'll just step this way, sir. Oh, you've changed your mind, sir?' she added in soulful tones as the man, his face suddenly gone chalk white, huddled back in his seat. 'What a pity, I'm sure they would really have *enjoyed* talking to you.' Deliberately she dropped the note on to his tray before turning to walk back to the galley amid the appreciative smiles and chuckles of the other passengers who had been interested onlookers of the little scene.

Lyn, too, had been watching from behind the curtain. 'Hey, that was really something! Where did you learn that trick?'

'It was one of the first lessons I had from my chief stewardess. I'd only been flying for about a month when someone made a really foul suggestion and I got mad and poured a drink over him. He reported me and I thought I'd get into a terrible row, but the chief stewardess just took me aside and told me about that ploy. Let's just hope he doesn't find out that the Captain is really an average-sized married man with four grown-up children!'

Lyn laughed. 'Well, he won't risk making a pass again at any rate.'

A voice crackled over the intercom from the flight deck. 'All right, Number One, you can settle them down for landing now. E.T.A. twenty minutes.'

Quickly the two girls stowed away everything that was

lying around loose in the galley, knowing that the two other stewardesses were doing the same in the economy class cabin. Genista picked up the cabin microphone and made the landing announcement, careful to keep exactly the right note of reassurance in her voice. 'Ladies and gentlemen, we hope you have enjoyed your flight with Globe Airways. We shall be arriving at Heathrow in approximately fifteen minutes. The weather in London is fine and we are on time. Please fasten your safety belts and extinguish all cigarettes. Thank you.' She had a light but warm voice with overtones of sexuality that flattered the male ego, yet with a sincerity that made her many friends among her fellow stewardesses.

Going forward to the crew's quarters, the girls took off their tabard aprons and made ready for landing. Genista tucked in a stray lock of her dark red hair that had escaped from the French pleat she always combed it into when working. Her clear green eyes, slightly shadowed now by tiredness, gazed back at her from under level brows. There was a glint of excited expect-ancy in her eyes as she thought of her date tonight with Paul Bryson. He was one of the senior co-pilots, hoping soon to be promoted to captain, and she had been out with him several times over the last two months. It was early days yet, of course, they were still at the pleasant stage of getting to know each other better, but Genista found that her pulse was beating rather faster at the thought of seeing him again, almost as much as he set her heart quivering every time he kissed her. She adjusted her cute little bowler hat on her head and pulled on her gloves before going to strap herself into her seat beside Lyn, facing down the cabin. The plane banked slightly as it lined up for the runway approach and then began a gradual descent. The giant tyres touched down smoothly on the runway and then the nose-wheel came down to join them as the reverse thrust of the engines slowed them down.

As Genista pushed open the door the cold, grey, early-morning air smelt good and clean after the close stuffiness of the cabin. The first passengers began to file past her and she bade them goodbye with her usual smile, even the man from seat F3, who glared at her balefully as he passed. A final check to make sure that no one had left anything behind and then the crew could hand over the plane to the ground staff. Once through the Customs check, Genista handed in her cash box and then she and the other stewardesses went to the Reconciliation Room where they made up their bar accounts, their tired brains making the effort to concentrate on this last job before they went home to sleep.

For once it worked out right first time and Genista gave a sigh of relief as she handed the accounts to the duty Ops. Officer. He glanced at it, but called her back as she went to turn away.

'Oh, no,' she said with a mock groan. 'I haven't made a mistake, have I?'

He grinned. 'No, it's not that. I've got a message for you. Here it is.' He took a message slip from his desk and handed it to her.

It was quite brief. 'Please phone Mr Kevin Grey in Paris urgently.' Genista gave a little moue of exasperation. Now what was Kevin up to? She toyed with leaving the call until she got to the flat, but the word 'urgently' glared back at her and she gave a rueful sigh before asking Lyn to wait while she made the call. Making her way to the nearest telephone booth, she gave the Paris number of Kevin's small flat. It would serve him right if she got him out of bed, she grumbled to herself as she waited for the connection. The bell seemed to ring for a long time, but when it was eventually answered she was surprised to hear, not her young brother's voice, but that of a woman, the concierge of the apartment house where her brother lived.

'*Ici* Mademoiselle Grey, *la soeur de* Monsieur Grey,' she began, but broke off as the woman interrupted her excitedly.

'*Votre frère n'est pas là, mademoiselle. Il a èté arrêté.*'

She continued to talk, but Genista stood numbly holding the receiver, the woman's high-pitched voice rolling over her. 'What—what did you say? That my brother has been arrested?' she managed to stammer out at last, forgetting in her shock to speak in French, so that she had to repeat herself. The concierge assured her it was true and this time Genista was able to function more coherently and learn that the police had taken Kevin away the previous evening. Almost automatically she wrote down the name of the Gendarmerie to which he'd been taken, her fingers seeming to move of their own accord, for her brain still wasn't working properly.

Replacing the receiver, she leant against the wall for a moment, forcing herself to calm down and try to think; the first thing she had to do was to get to Paris as quickly as possible and find out just why Kevin had been arrested. She remembered that a flight went out today that stopped at Paris to pick up passengers before flying on to India. Quickly she ran to the briefing board and saw that it left in less than thirty minutes. If only there was a spare seat! Running down the corridor she almost bumped into Lyn who was just coming to look for her.

'Oh, good, you've finished your call. Now we can go ...' But Lyn stopped as she saw her friend's distraught face. 'Why, Gen, what is it?'

'I have to get to Paris. Kevin's in trouble. Real trouble, Lyn.'

Lyn didn't delay her by asking questions, but immediately went with her to the Ops. Officer.

Fifteen minutes later, Genista was again hurrying across the tarmac, but this time to take her place as a passenger on a Boeing 747 jumbo jet. There had been several spare seats available as far as Paris and Lyn had wanted to come with her, but Genista had insisted on going alone, although promising to phone as soon as she knew anything definite. She was the last person on board, the stewardess closing the door as soon as she had stepped through it. It was almost with relief that she strapped herself into her seat, but soon she began to wonder anxiously what scrape Kevin had got himself into this time.

Kevin was just twenty, three years younger than herself, but to Genista those three years often felt like thirty, for it seemed that ever since she could remember she had been rescuing him from one scrape or another—not that he was mischievous, or even particularly adventurous—he was just accident-prone. His absorbing interest in life was inventing things, and once or twice they had paid off in a small way, although most of them had been spectacular failures. Genista still remembered with a shudder the time he had needed a length of tube so had calmly 'borrowed' the hose from the washing machine without telling her. They had been living in a second floor flat at the time and she had unknowingly switched on the machine one morning, leaving it to operate while she was at work. The ensuing floods of water had gone through the floor and brought down the ceiling of the flat below, completely ruining the carpets and furniture, with the result that Genista and Kevin had been thrown out of the flat and had to start house-hunting all over again.

The bond between brother and sister had always been a close one, mainly because their father had been a minor official in the Diplomatic Corps and had been sent to several European countries over the years. His family had accompanied him and he had insisted that Genista and Kevin should go to local schools to learn the language. This had drawn the two closer together until the people and things around them had lost their strangeness and they could understand their fellow pupils, but always after two or three years they had had to move on to another country and start all over again.

So it had been until just over four years ago when their parents had been killed in a skiing accident in Switzerland. By then Genista's education was complete, although it had been too broken to give her any high academic qualifications. It had, however, made her highly suitable for the one job she really wanted. There was something about flying that was absolutely fascinating to her; the thrill of the plane taking off, climbing miles up into the clear blueness of the sky, and then to land in a different hemisphere, a different world almost as she flew from winter to summer in just a few hours.

While Kevin had been still at school and college she had seen a lot of him, but nearly a year ago he had got himself a job in Paris in the offices of a Greek shipping firm, his ability to speak both French and Greek fluently having won him the post. Genista had been able to meet him several times during stopovers and he had seemed happy enough with his new job, but during the last few months he had been engrossed in a new invention that he was working on, and Kevin's biggest failing was that once he got absorbed in a project he tended to forget everything else!

The plane came crisply in to land at Orly Airport, the murky grey of the early morning giving way to a watery spring sunshine. The airport was busy with the influx of morning travellers and Genista was easily able to catch a taxi that had just dropped off a party. For a moment she toyed with the idea of going to Kevin's flat to see if he had been released, but decided instead to go straight to the Gendarmerie. She gave the address and sat impatiently as the driver made his way through the noisy rush hour traffic, no sooner breaking free of one hold-up before they were snarled up in another, so that it was almost an hour later when they arrived at her destination.

The gendarme on duty behind the high wooden counter greeted her politely and dashed all her hopes of a misunderstanding by telling her that Kevin was still held there. When she asked to see him she had to produce her passport as proof of her identity and was then interviewed by a more senior official before she was at last led down a long, white-painted corridor to a small, bare room containing only a table and two or three hard chairs by way of furniture. Here she was told to wait, and it wasn't until nearly ten nerve-racking minutes later that Kevin was at last ushered in.

Any feelings of anger or blame that Genista might have felt were instantly dispelled when she saw his face. He looked pale and tired, and very young. There were dark rings round his eyes as if he hadn't slept all night, and there was a tight, set look to his face, a look she hadn't seen since their parents' death when he had tried so hard to be an adult, to be as strong as a man. Quickly she went to him and hugged him; he was taller than she now and she had to reach up to ruffle his already untidy mop of hair, the same deep red as her own.

'Oh, Gen, I'm so glad you've come,' he said thickly, and then had to take out his handkerchief and blow his nose hard.

Genista took his hand and led him to a chair, talking lightly to give him time to recover himself, although her own voice was choked with emotion. 'You're all I've got, remember? When you send out S.O.S. signals then I come a-running like an old mother hen guarding her chick.'

Her simile made him give a weak grin and he was able to compose himself a little as he sat beside her at the table.

'Now, suppose you start by telling me what you've been accused of.'

'Embezzlement. But I didn't mean to steal the money, Gen, honestly I didn't!' he added in desperate appeal.

'Embezzlement?' She stared back at him appalled. His hands started to shake and he hurriedly doubled them into tight fists. Genista took a deep breath and reached out to cover his hands with her own. In as calm a voice as she could manage, she said, 'Kevin, we both know you didn't do it, so just begin at the beginning and tell me everything that happened in as much detail as you can.'

Slowly, stammeringly, at first, the story came out. 'It was this device I'd invented, you see. Working in the shipping agency had given me the idea for it. It's an electronic gadget that automatically checks the weight of a cargo as it's lowered into the holds.' He went on to explain the device in more technical terms, none of which Genista understood, but she let him go on talking about it because doing so seemed to help him to forget his predicament momentarily. 'Well, I had everything worked out in theory,' he went on, 'but of course I needed to test it practically. To do that meant having a prototype of the gadget made up at an electronics laboratory. I'd been looking round for a place for some time and had approached one or two, but they weren't interested, then I met a man, Jacques Fleuret, in a café and he knew someone who managed a laboratory with a very reputable firm. I told him all about my gadget and he seemed interested and promised to mention it to his friend. A few evenings later I met him by appointment and he said his friend would be willing to make up and test the device for me so long as it could be done within two weeks as his equipment was only free for that time. Another job had been delayed, or something. But he also said that the prototype had to be paid for in advance.

'Well, of course, that really threw me, because I didn't have any money.'

Genista accepted this without question; Kevin *never* had any money, he spent it all on scientific books and equipment.

'I'm afraid I hadn't given much thought to the financial side of it, but Monsieur Fleuret said that he would be willing to put up the money for a fifty per cent share in any profits the device made. I didn't like the idea very much, but it seemed the only way, so I agreed. But then, the day before we were due to start making the prototype, Fleuret phoned me at the office and said that his money had been delayed and wouldn't be available for another two days, which wouldn't have left enough time for the gadget to be made and tested. He suggested I borrow the money from someone. I was desperate, Gen! To have such wonderful luck and everything running smoothly and then to have it all go wrong at the last minute!' His eyes clouded as he remembered his disappointment.

'It seemed such a waste of all the months of work I'd put into it. That it should fall through for a measly sum of money.' His voice became a shade defiant as he continued, 'Well, I was making out the pay packets for the crew's wages of a ship that was due in three days' time, so I—well, I decided to borrow the money from the company. Fleuret had said his money would be through in two days, so I knew I could replace it before it was needed. I took the cash round to Fleuret straight away and he rushed off to his friend with it.'

He stopped as Genista gave a hollow groan. 'All right, you don't have to go on. I can imagine the rest.'

He nodded shamefacedly. 'Yes, I never saw Fleuret again. He'd left his lodgings, and when I checked with the electronics firm they said they'd never heard of him.'

'Oh, Kevin.' She shook her head at him in despair. 'What a mess!'

'I know. I'm sorry, Gen, but honestly, I didn't mean to steal the money. I meant to give it back,' he added, looking at her appealingly.

'Did you go to your firm and tell them what had happened?'

'I intended to, of course. I realised it was the only thing to do—but the worst part of it was that I took a day off to look for Fleuret and they found out the money was missing while I was away. They informed the police at once and I was arrested when I got back to the flat.'

'But didn't you tell them what happened?'

'Yes, of course I did,' Kevin answered with a trace of exasperation. 'But no one will believe me. They think I've either hidden the money, or else I had an accomplice who's done the dirty on me and gone off with the loot!'

Genista stared at him for a minute, her brain whirling as she tried to think what to do for the best, but then she noticed the half-scared, half-hopeful look on her brother's face and managed a bright, confident smile. 'Come on, cheer up. Don't look so glum. I'm sure we can sort the whole thing out before too long. I suppose the first thing is to see if we can get you out on bail, or whatever the equivalent is in France.'

Kevin shook his head. 'No good, I'm afraid. I asked them earlier. They think I'll do a bunk if they let me go.'

'Oh. Well—well, I shall just have to go and see your employers and explain the whole thing to them and offer to repay the money. You're sure to lose your job, of course, and probably get a good ticking off as well, but they surely won't prosecute if they've got their money back. Who at your office is the person to see?'

'The office manager is an old fogey called Blanchard, but he's under the directors and I don't expect he could make a decision like that himself.'

'Well, which of the directors, then?' Genista asked rather impatiently, eager now to get the whole hateful business over and done with.

'I'm not sure. They're all so high up in the company that they don't come to the office very often. The shipping company is only part of a really huge international organisation with interests in every kind of business. And besides, all the directors are at the beck and call of the owner and could be hard to get hold of.'

'The owner? Does just one man own all that, then?'

'Yes, his name's Marc Kiriakos. The shipping line and most of the international interests were left to him by his father, who was a Greek, but he also inherited vast areas of land in France through his mother's family. They say he rules the company with a rod of iron and knows everything that goes on. Everything tightens up when he's in Paris. That's probably why they found out that I'd borrowed the money so quickly.'

Genista leaned forward. 'You mean he's in Paris at the moment?'

Kevin nodded. 'Yes, he came here for some conference or other.'

'Then he's the person I shall have to talk to,' she said decisively.

With mouth agape, Kevin stared at her speechlessly for a moment. Then, 'The old man! But—but you can't see him!'

'Why not?'

'Because—well, because he's who he is, that's why not. It would be like trying to walk into Buckingham Palace and see the Queen! You wouldn't get past the first secretary. And it wouldn't be any good trying to be persuasive; everyone's too scared of him to go against his wishes.'

'Nevertheless I'm going to try. I've found that if you really want to get something done or put right, then the best thing to do is to go to the man at the top, preferably when they're away from the office because they're more vulnerable in their own homes. Where does this Marc Kiriakos stay in Paris?'

For the first time Kevin gave a slight grin. 'In a penthouse on the top of the company building.'

'Oh.' Genista looked slightly dashed, but recovered. 'Well, I'll just have to beard the lion in his den, won't I?' She smiled and gave him a hug. 'Keep your chin up. We'll have you out of here in next to no time.'

But although Genista had spoken so reassuringly, she took a taxi to the shipping line with a sinking heart. It was going to take every ounce of persuasion she possessed to convince his employer that he hadn't any criminal intentions. This Monsieur Kiriakos sounded like a real martinet who ruled his business empire out of fear rather than respect, and it hardly seemed likely that he would take a lenient view of Kevin's escapade, despite his previous good character. Still, she *had* to try. She just couldn't let Kevin spend what could possibly be years of his youth in some horrid jail. She would do anything rather than let that happen.

It was only a short ride to the offices of the shipping line and Genista gave a gasp of surprise when she got out of the taxi. Situated in one of the best business areas, it was an immense white building that soared high into the sky, the late April sunshine reflecting off the hundreds of plate glass windows. Genista stared, then squared her shoulders; she would get to see Marc Kiriakos if she had to fight her way up every floor!

And three hours later it almost seemed as if she had! From her first, 'Good morning, I should like to see Monsieur Kiriakos on a personal matter,' she had met with shocked stares and brusque attempts to get rid of her, but she had resolutely stood her ground and had politely repeated her name and her request. Gradually she had been passed upwards, both physically up the building and also through the hierarchy of the company.

Individuals of ever greater importance had tried to send her away or to find out what she wanted. She had refused to say why she was there, refused to talk to anyone but Monsieur Kiriakos. The men had stared at her, talked between themselves for a while and then left her sitting patiently in a chair (back straight, legs crossed at the ankles, hands in her lap, as she had been taught at stewardess training school) while they had gone off to confer with someone else, until eventually she had been escorted slightly higher up the building to go through the whole thing again.

Her stubborn refusal to explain had carried her up to the floor below the penthouse, and here she again sat down to wait in a beautifully designed, very modern leather armchair. This floor, she gathered, was given over to the offices of the great man himself, and, if this lobby was anything to go by, he was also a very rich one. The floor was fitted with a vast expanse of deep-pile grey carpet, on the walls were several pictures by contemporary artists, cubists and abstracts, and here and there were some pieces of modern sculpture in marble and bronze. It was all very progressive, very expensive.

Genista resolutely tried to make herself relax in the chair, but her nerves were jangling and she soon sat forward again, her hands twisting in her lap. At the other end of the lobby, by a massive double door, two male secretaries sat at desks at least three yards wide, and eyed her covertly whenever they thought she wasn't looking. You didn't have to be psychic to imagine the thoughts that were going through their heads, the interpretation they were putting on her refusal to explain her visit. Her tummy made protesting sounds as she moved restlessly in the chair and she realised that she hadn't eaten anything except a light 'in-flight' meal shortly after taking off from Hong Kong the previous day. She had expected to cook herself a proper breakfast with Lyn at the flat and so hadn't bothered with the breakfast provided by the airline. Tiredness swept over her suddenly and she leant back against the chair. She had dozed a little on the plane, but always found it impossible to sleep properly while on duty; she was always half-listening for a buzz from one of the passengers, ready to hurry to answer it before it woke anyone else. Jet lag, too, didn't help, but the worst part was this waiting around, always waiting, when she so much wanted to get the whole thing over.

For the tenth time she glanced at her watch; one-thirty and she'd been sitting there for nearly three-quarters of an hour now. She gave a weary sigh; she had never felt less like fighting a battle, but she knew that Kevin was relying on her, had an implicit faith that she would rescue him once again. And she couldn't let him go to jail; she'd beggar herself rather than do that. Impatiently she tapped her foot on the floor; if the old Croesus didn't hurry up and see her she would wear a hole in his precious carpet!

But there was another half hour still to wait before a buzzer sounded discreetly at one of the desks and the elder of the two secretaries walked across the lobby towards her.

'If you will follow me, mademoiselle, Monsieur Kiriakos will give you five minutes of his time, but no longer, you understand?'

Genista stood up and stared at him for a moment before swallowing and then nodding her head. It would take an awful lot of persuasion to get what she wanted in five minutes, but she was certainly going to try!

The secretary led her across the lobby and opened one of the double doors. He gave her a slight bow as she passed him to stand hesitantly in the doorway. Then she straightened her shoulders and lifted her head up high, chin defiantly forward. After all, he couldn't eat her, could he? Boldly she stepped into the room, her feet sinking into an even deeper carpet. The door closed quietly behind her. To her surprise the office was sparsely furnished, without any of the usual filing cabinets, photo-copiers or other business impedimenta, just a huge, modern desk only slightly smaller than Salisbury Plain and a communications console. At one end of the room there was a big picture window giving a breathtaking panoramic view of Paris which rivalled that of the Eiffel Tower. A man was standing with his back to her, gazing out of the window across the rooftops. He turned slowly to look at her and Genista braced herself to meet old man Croesus himself.

A surge of anger filled her as the man came towards her; she had thought she was going to see Monsieur Kiriakos at last, but they must have just passed her up another rung of the ladder, for this man was much too young. Only in his mid-thirties, he was over six feet tall, slim and easy in his movements. His eyebrows were as dark as his thick, wavy hair, eyebrows that were raised slightly as he regarded her coldly. His clothes, his air, were unmistakably French, and he had a look of intense virility and yet sophistication, a sort of powerful, care-less charm that can be quite devastating.

Stiffly she said in French, 'I'm sorry. I've obviously been brought to the wrong office. I wanted to see Mon-sieur Kiriakos.'

The man continued to look at her, running his dark grey eyes over her slim figure, noticing her uniform with the one-winged badge of a stewardess and the tiny gold star showing her rank marking. He sat down in the high-backed chair on the other side of the desk. 'I am Marc Kiriakos.'

'Oh!' Genista stared. 'I thought you would be much. . . .' She broke off hurriedly.

'Not all business heads are old men, Mademoiselle Grey,' he said drily, and Genista realised that he had spoken in faultless English. 'You're wasting time,' he added curtly. 'Sit down and tell me what you want of me.'

Hastily Genista slipped into a chair opposite him, a much harder one than the chair outside in the lobby —evidently Monsieur Kiriakos didn't encourage his visitors to stay long! Trying not to look at the hard, un-prepossessing set of his mouth, she began nervously, 'I don't suppose you know anything about it, but my brother works for you, or at least he did, but unfortunately there was a terrible misunderstanding and he's been blamed for doing something he didn't mean to do. What I mean is . . . well, he's really very young and he —sometimes he gets carried away, but he really doesn't mean any harm and he. . . .' Her own voice sounded high-pitched and muddled even to her own ears and she broke off miserably as she looked into the cold, dark eyes that looked across at her so contemptuously.

'You are mistaken, mademoiselle,' Marc Kiriakos said sarcastically. 'I am fully aware of your brother and the crime he has committed. The embezzlement was brought to my notice immediately and it was by my order that he was arrested.'

'But you don't understand,' Genista said desperately. 'He wasn't stealing the money. He fully intended to re- pay it, but he was tricked by a con-man who ran off with the money. He knows it was wrong and he's extremely sorry, but I'm fully prepared to repay the sum out of my own pocket so that you won't have lost anything.'

'Keep your money, Mademoiselle Grey. I don't tolerate thieves in my employ and I intend to see that your brother receives the full punishment for his crime!'

Genista stared at him. 'But you can't be so cruel, so vindictive. Kevin's only twenty, he's just a boy!'

His hard jawline tightened slightly. 'You're wasting your time if you think you can appeal to my sympathy, mademoiselle. Your brother was old enough to know what he was doing and he will have to take the con- sequences. And you aren't doing him any favours by trying to protect him from his folly. Eventually he'll have to learn to face the outcome of his own actions. He can't hide behind your skirts for ever,' he added with heavy sarcasm.

Genista found that she had risen to her feet. She was appalled by this man's casual destruction of her brother's life, his despotic contempt of her pleas. She felt herself shaking with emotion as fatigue and anger overwhelmed her. She saw that he was stretching out a hand to the console on his desk to buzz to have her shown out. Al- most of its own volition her arm came out and knocked his hand away.

'Oh, no, you don't!' she said furiously. 'If you think I've waited in this concrete monstrosity for over four hours just to be thrown out after five minutes, then you're wrong! You may play at being God Almighty to those unfortunate people who rush to obey your every order because you've frightened the guts out of them, but I'm not afraid of you! I'm not afraid to tell you that you're cruel and mean and spiteful! But I suppose that's how you've got to be when you're in your position, isn't it?' It was Genista's turn to be sarcastic now. 'I suppose I should really feel sorry for you; sorry that you have to stab people in the back, make enemies, bankrupt small companies, put people out of work, to get where you are. Because I bet that's how you did it. I bet you haven't got a friend in the world!'

His hands gripped the arms of his chair, his eyes were like cold steel and there was a hard, set look to his mouth, but he didn't attempt to stop her or, surprisingly, to press the buzzer. He merely stared up at her while she continued to rant at him, her temper completely lost.

'My brother makes one mistake, and rather than let me put it right, you take out your vindictive spite on him. Ruin his life before it's hardly begun. Well, don't think that I'm going to sit back tamely and take it. I'm going to hire the best lawyer in Paris to defend him, and I'll make sure your name gets dragged in as much mud as I can!' She was shaking with rage, blinking back tears of anger and frustration. She balled her hands into fists and wished fervently that she were a man so that she could hit him. 'I'll make you *wallow* in mud before I'm through! My God, if having more money than you can count means being like you, then I hope I never have a fraction of your wealth!' Still trembling with fury, she said scornfully, 'All right, you can send for your lackey to open the door. I've said all I'm ever going to say to you.'

The silence after she had finished seemed to fill the room as much as her raised voice had done. She expected him to press the buzzer and have her thrown out at once, but he still sat rigidly in the chair, then he seemed to relax a little and surprised her by saying slowly, 'You're very—loyal, Mademoiselle Grey.'

Suddenly her anger was spent and fatigue swept over her in waves. 'Kevin is all I've got,' she said tiredly, and lifted a hand to her forehead that had begun to throb unmercifully.

Marc Kiriakos leaned forward. 'Did you fly here this morning?'

'Yes.' Somehow the question didn't seem incongruous. 'I was given the message as soon as we landed and I came straight here.'

'Landed?'

'I was on an overnight flight from Hong Kong.' Turning away, she said, 'I'll go now.' She stumbled a little as she walked towards the heavy doors. To her surprise and dismay, he came behind her and caught her arm to steady her. She hadn't even heard him move! Quickly she tried to jerk away. 'I've said I'm going. You don't have to throw me out personally,' she added bitterly.

But he didn't let go of her arm. 'When did you last eat?'

'What's that to you?' Genista glared up at him. The cold, harsh look had left his eyes; they were still dark, but they weren't completely impersonal. She gave up trying to read them and looked away.

'I was just about to have a rather belated lunch before I was told that you wanted to see me,' he told her drily. 'I think you'd better join me before you pass out on your feet.'

'Eat with you? I'd rather have lunch with a boa-constrictor!' She tried to wrench her arm away again, but he held it firmly.

He raised his left eyebrow quizzically. 'You could always make use of the time to tell me how your brother managed to get himself into so much trouble.'

Genista's jaw dropped. She goggled at him. For a second a look that might have been amusement came into his eyes but was quickly suppressed. He drew her towards a section of wall that contained a concealed lift and she mutely allowed herself to be led into it, too overcome with amazement to disobey him.

The lift was so smooth and silent that she didn't realise they were moving until the doors opened and she stepped into his penthouse apartment. It was a lovely room, straight out of the latest edition of *Ideal Penthouse*, decorated in shades of grey and with the very newest of luxurious furniture, but somehow it had a lived-in look about it—possibly because of the richly coloured French Impressionist paintings, the shelves of books and the huge record and cassette collection that filled a whole wall.

Monsieur Kiriakos pointed towards a door over on the right. 'There's a bathroom beyond the bedroom through there, if you'd like to freshen up. Lunch will be served in ten minutes.'

'Th-thank you.' Genista still found it hard to accept the sudden change in his attitude. She went through to the sumptuous but very masculine bedroom. The bed was huge! She couldn't resist taking a closer look at it. Beneath the zebra-skin bedspread there were black silk sheets. Wow! She blinked, and wondered just what kind of entertaining Marc Kiriakos did in his penthouse pad. She was willing to bet it wasn't always his wife, if the business tycoons she'd come across during her work were anything to go by. They always seemed to be travelling with their 'secretaries' or 'nieces' who were invariably young and gorgeous.

The bathroom was so beautiful it made her drool; a sunken bath made out of black marble and big enough for at least three people, gold-plated fittings, and mirrors everywhere! She was beginning to suspect that she had stumbled into the nest of a proverbial playboy, although that image didn't seem to go with her first impression of him as a ruthless business tycoon. As she washed her hands and touched up her make-up, she tried to puzzle out the reason for his sudden reversal after she'd shouted at him. Did it mean that he might give Kevin a second chance? Well, at least he'd said he would listen. She must just hang on to that and do her best to put her brother's case. Having tidied her hair, she didn't replace her hat but carried it in her hand as she walked through the bedroom and into the big living-room. It felt rather as if she was going into the second round of a very uneven fight after almost having been knocked out in the first!

CHAPTER TWO

THE room was split-level, and a small table had been set for lunch on the upper level close to the patio doors opening on to a roof garden, but now the doors were closed, for the April sunshine hadn't yet enough warmth in it to encourage eating out in the open. Marc Kiriakos pulled out a chair for her and to her surprise proceeded to serve her himself from a heated trolley.

As he placed a plate of hors d'oeuvres before her he noticed her surprise and said, 'I usually have a working lunch and prefer to serve myself.' He sat down opposite her and filled her glass with claret from a bottle with a famous label that she'd heard about but had never imagined herself drinking. 'I hope the wine is to your taste.'

Almost reverently Genista lifted the glass to her lips and sipped it. 'It's perfect,' she admitted in rather an awed voice. 'The best I've ever tasted. Even better than I thought it would be.'

'You know about wines?'

'All the stewardesses have to go on a gourmet's course to learn about wines and food before they're allowed to work on international routes,' she answered, and then flushed slightly as she realised that he was watching her intently.

'Then I hope you also approve my choice of food.'

They began to eat and Genista found her spirits reviving rapidly. At first they ate in silence, but after he had brought her the second course he began to question her closely about herself.

'Your brother was employed in my offices because he could speak Greek as well as French and English. Do you also speak Greek?'

'Yes, we lived in Athens for nearly three years.'

He looked at her interrogatively so Genista went on to explain about their background. He seemed interested and asked her how long she had been working for the airline and whether she enjoyed the work.

'I love it,' she said with unconcealed enthusiasm, her eyes bright, the colour having come back into her cheeks now. 'It gives you a sense of freedom, a feeling that you've broken all the laws of gravity and time.'

She would have gone on to say more, but noticed a slight frown between his straight brows. Evidently this had been the wrong thing to say, so she hastily changed the subject. 'You—you said I could tell you about Kevin,' she began rather nervously.

'You're very tenacious, mademoiselle.' His eyes were cold again, but he intimated that she should go on. By the time she had finished her story they had eaten dessert and he had poured out coffee and lit a cigarette. For a while he was silent, not looking at her, just sitting back in his chair watching the smoke drifting up towards the ceiling. At length he lowered his head, his dark, rather heavy-lidded eyes regarding her almost detachedly.

'Mademoiselle Grey, do you know how much your brother—borrowed?'

Genista shook her head. 'No, I forgot to ask him, but I have some savings and I'm sure I can....'

Brusquely he interrupted her. 'It was a hundred thousand francs. That's about ten thousand pounds in ster-ling.'

She felt as if she'd been turned to stone; her heart seemed to have stopped beating and her blood felt like ice in her veins. She had had no idea it was such a large amount, thinking it was only a few hundred pounds. 'He —he said it was a measly sum,' she stammered at last.

'Your brother obviously has no conception of the value of money,' Marc Kiriakos said grimly. 'Do I take it that you are unable to repay it, after all?'

'No, I'm—afraid I can't.' Genista looked down at her hands on the table, twisting and pleating the soft linen of her napkin.

'You said that your brother was all you had; am I to take it that there is no one from whom you can borrow the money? A relative—or a friend?'

Slowly she shook her head. 'No, there's no one.'

'You don't have a fiancé or boy-friend who would lend it to you?'

For a moment she hesitated, the thought of Paul filling her mind. But how could she go to him and ask him for such a huge sum so early in their friendship? Even if he had it and was willing to lend it to her, it would bring an impossible awkwardness into any future re-lationship they might have. Silently she shook her head again.

'In that case, mademoiselle, you have been deliberately wasting my time,' her host said callously. 'You can hardly expect me to withdraw the charges against your brother when there is absolutely no possibility of pay-ing the money involved.'

Genista raised her eyes to his pleadingly. 'If you'll just give me time I promise you that I'll repay every penny.'

But his eyes were like ice again, his face stern and un-sympathetic. God, she thought, doesn't the man ever smile? She tried one last desperate plea. 'Please, Mon-sieur Kiriakos, don't send my brother to prison!'

Without looking directly at her, he leaned forward to crush out his cigarette, then slowly sat back in his chair, his hands resting casually on the arms. 'There is, perhaps, one way....' he began thoughtfully.

'Yes?' Genista sat forward eagerly, her hands gripping the edge of the table, hope rising in her heart.

'The sum could possibly be worked off over a period of time.'

'You mean you'd let Kevin pay it back out of his salary? Why, that's marvellous! Oh, Monsieur Kiriakos, I don't know how to thank....'

But he held up a hand and interrupted her. 'No, that is not what I mean. I have no intention of keeping your brother in my employ; to do so would be unfair on the rest of my staff—the ones who don't "borrow" money.' He rose and went over to a drinks cabinet where he poured himself out a cognac. Then he came to sit opposite her again, twisting the delicate stem of the glass between his fingers. 'No, Mademoiselle Grey, the idea I had in mind was that you should pay off the debt by filling a—vacant post in my organisation.'

Genista stared at him. 'Me? You—you're offering me a job?' Gropingly she tried to cope with this new turn of events. Kevin had said that Marc Kiriakos was an international tycoon, but she had no idea he owned an airline. It was more likely, though, that he had his own private jet and perhaps wanted her for that. 'You need a stewardess?' she asked tentatively.

He shook his head. 'Hardly. Let me explain; I find it

necessary to do a great deal of entertaining and my guests
are from every country in the world. It would be useful
for me to have someone who speaks several languages,
who is experienced in meeting and dealing with people
of importance, to help me on these occasions. From what
you have told me of your background, it would seem that
you are entirely suited to cope with such a position. Well,
mademoiselle?' he added somewhat impatiently when
she didn't answer straightaway.

'You mean—give up flying?' she asked slowly.

'But of course. I've already said that I don't require a
glorified waitress, but I do need a hostess.'

'A sort of social secretary?'

'Rather more than that, mademoiselle,' he said drily.
'The position I am offering is that of my wife.'

Genista literally couldn't believe her ears. She stared
across the table to where he sat so calmly, just as if he
hadn't made the most startling proposal she was ever
likely to hear! 'Could—could you say that again, please?'
she asked faintly.

'I asked you to be my wife,' he replied without any
apparent emotion in his expression.

'But there must be lots of women who would give their
right arm to.... That is—I mean, there must be lots of
girls that you....' She broke off in some embarrassment,
then added with a rush, 'But you don't *know* me.'

'I know enough about you to realise that you would
be suitable for my purposes,' he said in a cold, dry voice.
'As you say, there are a great many women of my own
class and position from whom I could choose a wife; I'm
continually beset by women who want to interest me in
their daughters, or by ambitious girls who throw themselves at my head. It is partly to spare me from these that

I need a wife, but if I were to choose one of them she would demand my constant attention, would expect me to escort her wherever it took her fancy to show herself off. But I have neither the time nor the wish to play the doting husband,' he added with a wry twist to his mouth. 'I need someone on hand to perform the duties of a wife and then to keep out of my way. Almost a business relationship, in fact. Do I make myself clear, mademoiselle?'

'Yes, quite clear.'

'You did not, I hope, imagine that I had fallen head over heels in love with your charms?' he added sarcastically.

Genista coloured and shot him an angry look across the table. 'No, of course I didn't,' she answered tartly. She tried to gather her scattered wits and to think the thing through. 'If you'd just wanted a social secretary—but marriage! I couldn't, I just couldn't.' She spread her hands helplessly, the enormity of the idea overwhelming her.

He shrugged. 'Very well, mademoiselle, the choice is yours. But I was under the impression that you wanted to save your brother from prison.'

'I do! You know I do. But this....' She bit her lip and looked at him pleadingly. 'Surely there must be some other way?'

He shook his head decisively. 'No, there is no other way.'

Agitatedly Genista stood up and began to walk around the room, then came back to grip the back of her chair with trembling hands, thoughts of everything she would have to give up whirling through her brain. 'Please—I must have time to think.'

He looked up at her for a long moment, his expression inscrutable, then he glanced down at his watch. 'Very well,' he said at last. 'I have to go to a meeting that will last approximately two hours. When I return I shall expect an answer, is that understood?'

She nodded dumbly and he rose and crossed to the lift. He looked back at her before stepping into it and for a moment their glances locked, then he turned away and the doors closed silently behind him.

Slowly Genista walked down the steps into the lower part of the room, her thoughts a chaotic jumble as she tried to get the situation clear in her mind. Her first reaction was to say no, no, no! To be constantly in the company of this cold, unfeeling man was the last thing she wanted, however businesslike the relationship. He had seemed so cold-blooded, so emotionless about the whole thing, just as if he was discussing a business merger. Had he no normal masculine feelings about the woman he wanted to marry? Surely he must have felt something for some woman in the past? And marriage was such an irrevocable step!

She crossed to the picture window and opened it to go out into the roof garden. From here the noise of the traffic below was just a faint hum, hardly noisier than the song of the birds that were flying from their nests built in the branches of a lemon tree. As she sat down on a stone seat beneath the dazzling pink beauty of a weeping cherry tree in full bloom, her thoughts turned to Paul. She had a date with him tonight; he would come to call for her at eight o'clock, tall and fair and dashingly handsome. They would go to a small, intimate restaurant to eat and then on to a night-club to dance until the small hours. He would hold her close in his arms while they danced and, if Lyn was out or in bed when they got back, come up to the flat where he would kiss her goodnight, kiss her until her heart raced and she was quiveringly, excitingly aware of him.

How could she bear to give him up? If she left now, she could hurry to the airport and catch a plane to London, could be back in time to go out with him to-night. Leave all this behind her. Distractedly she began to walk along a path between beds of spring flowers, the yellow of daffodils, the deep red of early tulips. But if she ran away she would be leaving Kevin to stand his trial and an almost certain conviction. She was clear-headed enough to see that even the best advocate in Paris wouldn't stand a chance against Marc Kiriakos' huge organisation once it was brought to bear, and she had no illusions left now, no hopes of persuading him to be lenient or merciful. He was a hard, implacable man and if she refused to do what he wanted she knew that he wouldn't hesitate to make an example of her brother.

She supposed that in a way she ought to be grateful to him for giving her this one opportunity of keeping Kevin out of prison, but there was little gratitude in her heart. Instead it was filled with bitterness and anger; inevitably anger against Kevin for having been weak and stupid enough to have got himself in this mess, and bitterness against Marc Kiriakos who could so easily have been magnanimous over what to him must be a trifling sum, but who had instead used moral blackmail to try to get her to agree to marry him. And what a marriage to look forward to! To be brought out and made use of on social occasions and then made to disappear into the background until the next time she was wanted. Rather like a lace tablecloth she remembered her grandmother using—brought out only when guests were coming to tea and then folded up and put away in the cupboard again, she thought with bitter irony.

And his mistresses? Would she also be expected to turn a blind eye whenever he brought a woman back to that huge bed with the black sheets? The thought revolted her, but she was too experienced in the ways of business-men to imagine that Marc Kiriakos was different from any other. He was fabulously rich, still young, and darkly attractive. He had said himself that women flocked round him, and she could well believe it.

The path ended at an ornamental fishpond where a small waterfall made a musical, tinkling sound in this quiet place. Genista sat down on a convenient lump of rock and stared at the goldfish that skittered among the waterlilies. He must have known all along that she had no choice but to marry him, but it had taken her some time to accept the fact. Well, if she had to marry him then she would just have to make the best of it, but nowadays marriage didn't have to be such an irreversible step as it once had been, and there were some terms of her own that she intended to stipulate.

He came back earlier than he had said, coming straight out into the garden to look for her. She heard his quick footsteps from where she still sat by the goldfish pool, but didn't call out or go to meet him. He ducked under a branch of a budding lilac tree and came to an abrupt halt when he saw her. 'So there you are.' A flicker of some-thing that could have been relief showed in his face for a second and then was quickly gone.

Slowly Genista got to her feet and turned to face him.

'Have you come to a decision?' he asked.

'Not entirely. There are one or two questions I should

like to ask you before I finally make up my mind.' He nodded, and she went on, 'If I agree to your proposal, what would become of my brother?'

'I will arrange for the charges against him to be dropped and he will be released at once. I think perhaps it would be better if he went abroad. I have large business interests in Australia and, if you are agreeable, I would arrange for him to be given a post there and he could fly out almost immediately.'

'I see.' And she could, all too clearly, that he didn't want any relation of hers making inconvenient claims on her time or being a possible source of embarrassment to him. But in this case it suited her, too. 'Would Kevin have to know that I was married to you?'

His eyes narrowed. 'Not if you didn't want him to.'

She nodded slightly and said slowly, 'Then I have just one final question. If I refuse—if I don't marry you— how long a sentence would Kevin get?'

He turned away from her and walked across to lean against the brick parapet surrounding the roof before shrugging his shoulders and saying almost casually, 'About seven years, I should think, although the fact that it is his first offence might possibly reduce it to five.'

'Five years! So long?' Quickly she swung round and turned her back on him, unwilling to let him see the dismay in her face. It was such a long, long time.

'Well, have you made up your mind?' His voice came harshly behind her.

Genista straightened her shoulders and turned a white, set face towards him. He was still leaning against the parapet, his hands in his pockets, but his eyes regarded her intently and there was a steely alertness behind his outwardly casual manner. Defiantly she lifted her chin. 'Yes, I have. I will marry you, Monsieur Kiriakos, but as it seems that I am to serve my brother's sentence for him, then I will only serve the term he would have received. I will marry you for five years and not a day longer!'

For a long moment he didn't move, didn't change his expression, then he said slowly, 'Very well, mademoiselle, that would seem to be a fair decision.' Then he added in a more businesslike tone, 'But there will be an option to renew the contract if both sides are agreeable at the end of that time.' He raised an eyebrow and there was a ghost of a smile at the corner of his mouth as he said, 'Who knows—you may even get to like the job.' He came forward and took her arm. 'It's getting chilly out here. Shall we go inside and discuss this further?'

Docilely Genista allowed him to escort her inside the penthouse; she felt strangely numb now that the decision had finally been made. He poured her out a drink and gave it to her.

'Perhaps we should drink a toast to our,' he hesitated, 'liaison?'

Genista nodded dully and lifted the glass to her lips— it was champagne.

'I think it best that we should be married as soon as possible. A civil ceremony, of course, in a quiet place outside Paris.'

Moving across to a long, low settee, Genista sat down and tried to concentrate on what he was saying. His manner seemed different now, there was almost a lightness in his step and voice. 'My brother——' she interrupted him.

'Of course.' He stepped across to the telephone and spoke into it for several minutes before putting the receiver down and crossing to sit beside her, his arm negligently lying along the back of the settee. 'That's all taken care of; your brother will be released as soon as the necessary formalities are completed and I've arranged for him to contact you as soon as he's free.'

'Thank you,' Genista said rather stiltedly. She found his presence so close to her rather overpowering and edged further away along the seat.

Marc Kiriakos watched her for a moment and there was a sarcastic curl to his lips as he rose and went to sit in another chair.

Genista flushed and said hurriedly, 'I'm really very grateful, Monsieur Kiriakos. After I've spoken to Kevin I'll go straight back to London and give in my notice to Globe Airways.'

Coldly he said, 'Keep your gratitude—I intend to see that your brother's debt is repaid in full. And there is no necessity for you to go back to London; fortunately I own considerable shares in your airline and I have given orders for them to be contacted so that you can leave their employ immediately.'

She stared at him, hardly able to keep up with the speed at which he moved. 'But—but I shall have to go back,' she stammered. 'I have to collect my things and tell my flatmate. I can't just. . . .'

'Is your flat on the telephone?'

'Yes.'

'Then I suggest you call your friend and ask her to pack your personal possessions, and then, if you will give me the address, I will see that they are collected and brought here. But there is no need to bother about your clothes.'

A stubborn look came into Genista's face. 'And just

what is wrong with my clothes?'

He raised an eyebrow. 'Nothing, I imagine. Presumably you have good taste, but I must remind you that you will be moving among the best dressed women in the world and you will have to dress as befits my wife,' he said caustically. 'I will open accounts for you with all the leading couture houses and you can choose what you want from them,' he added.

Stunned into silence, Genista could only stare at him, then she pulled herself together, swallowed, and said rather faintly, 'Monsieur Kiriakos, I....'

He interrupted her. 'Don't you think that as we are to be married we could, perhaps, call each other by our christian names? Mine is Marc.'

'Yes. Yes, I know.' She stood up and walked rather aimlessly across to the bookcase before turning to face him again. 'This is all happening so quickly! You—you'll have to give me some time to adjust.'

He stood up and came casually across to stand beside her. 'There will be plenty of time to adjust, as you call it, after we are married. Now that we have come to a decision I can see no possible reason for delay,' he said brusquely. 'Now, I have some business to attend to that will take me about half an hour, so I will leave you to telephone your friend. I think it would be better at the moment if you don't tell her of our plans; I abhor unnecessary publicity and I would prefer to keep our wedding as quiet as possible.' He indicated the telephone. 'If you give my secretary your number in London he will put it through for you.'

'Thank you.' Genista watched him go, but didn't move to pick up the telephone straightaway. She felt dizzy and out of control of herself, as if she was sitting on an endless helter-skelter that went round and round at an ever-increasing speed. The way in which he seemed to have suddenly taken her life in his hands and was manipulating it as he wished took her breath away. All the normal course of events that she had anticipated; working out a month's notice, packing her belongings, explaining and saying goodbye to Lyn—and to Paul—all these had just been swept aside as a mere bagatelle. She supposed that eventually she might get used to living at such a pace, but just now her tired mind and body just weren't able to cope with it.

At length she roused herself to pick up the phone and give the number of the flat. Lyn answered almost at once and gave a gasp of relief when she heard Genista's voice.

'Gen! I've been wondering what on earth had happened to you. Where are you?'

'I'm still in Paris. Lyn,' she began awkwardly, 'something has cropped up and I won't be coming back to London.'

'Not today, you mean?'

'No, I mean I won't be coming back at all. You see, the only way I could get Kevin out of trouble was to take a job that his boss offered me. It means I'll have to give up flying and stay in Paris.'

'What? But how can you possibly? And surely you'll have to come back here? Gen, what's *happened*?' Lyn's voice rose in alarm.

'I'm sorry, but I can't explain everything now,' Genista said rather desperately, knowing just what her outspoken flatmate would have to say if she knew the truth. 'Would you please pack my things for me—and my clothes,' she added with a trace of defiance in her voice. 'Someone will call to collect them for me. And—and Lyn.' Her voice slowed. 'Will you see Paul? Tell him I'm sorry, but—but I won't be able to see him again.'

'Gen!' Lyn's voice almost exploded across the wires. 'Genista Grey, if you don't tell me what's happening this minute, then I'll get on the first plane and come over there myself.'

'Lyn, I can't. I'm sorry. I'll write to you and arrange for us to meet the next time you have a stopover in Paris. I'll explain everything then. Goodbye, Lyn.' And she put the phone down hurriedly, her friend's voice still echoing in her ear.

She felt terribly tired and longed to curl up on the settee and go to sleep, but she forced herself to go into the bathroom to wash and put on new make-up. Afterwards she felt refreshed and better able to to face the rest of the day, but, passing through the bedroom, she couldn't help wondering where she would be spending the night.

When Marc came back again she was sitting on the settee in apparent composure, flicking through a magazine. 'You have made your call?' When she nodded, he went on, 'Then I think it's time we left here. Shall we go?'

When they were in the rapidly descending lift, she asked, 'Where are we going?'

'I'm taking you to stay with an aunt of mine, Madame de Frémond. She has an apartment in the Rue Fontaine. You will stay with her until our marriage.'

In no time at all, it seemed to Genista, she had been whisked across Paris in a sleek Rolls-Royce and ushered into a luxurious apartment on the third floor of what had once been a mansion of the French nobility. She hadn't quite known what to expect his aunt to be like, but the woman who came forward to greet her was short and thin, grey-haired, and dressed in a very chic, very expensive outfit that shouted 'Dior' with every swirl of the beautifully cut skirt.

'Welcome to my home, mademoiselle,' Madame de Frémond greeted her lightly, then added, 'But, Marc, what are you thinking of? The poor child looks quite worn out.' She led Genista into a drawing-room where a fire was burning in a beautiful old fireplace and saw her seated in a comfortable armchair beside it before she left her to talk to Marc who was waiting in the hallway.

She was gone a long time and Genista guessed that Marc must be telling her about his plans. Marc! It seemed so odd that she now had to think of this stranger by his first name. Somehow she didn't think she would ever get used to it. The room was warm and cosy, the curtains drawn against the cool of the evening. Before very long Genista's head began to nod and soon she had fallen asleep, her head resting on the wing of the gold brocade chair.

She was awakened by a light touch on her arm and looked up to see Madame de Frémond standing over her, a sympathetic smile on her face. Genista flushed and straightened up hurriedly. 'Oh, I'm so sorry. I must have dropped off.'

'Which was hardly surprising when you haven't slept for so long. I suggest that we have dinner now and that you then go to bed straightaway so that you will be fresh for the morning.'

She led the way into a panelled dining-room and chattered amiably as they ate, talking of Paris and the latest fashions. 'Marc has asked me to take you round the fashion houses tomorrow so that you can select your trousseau.' (Ordered, more likely, Genista thought privately.) 'We need only choose what you need for your immediate requirements. You can select your other things for yourself when you have more time.'

Genista was glad to let her prattle on, grateful that she didn't have to make conversation while her mind was in such a whirl, and even more grateful that Madame de Frémond didn't ask her any questions about herself; the last thing she wanted at the moment was to face an inquisition from her hostess.

Just as they finished dinner, a maid came to tell her that there was a telephone call for her and showed her into a small, mirrored salon where she left her alone. Eagerly Genista picked up the receiver and was over-whelmed with an intense feeling of relief as she heard Kevin's voice.

'Gen? Is that you?'

'Yes. Are you all right? Did they let you go?'

'Yes, I'm back at my flat. I don't know how you worked it, but thanks, Sis. I was beginning to think I was never going to get out of that hell-hole.'

She laughed rather weakly, the happiness in his voice reward enough. Then she asked tentatively, 'Did who-ever came to get you say anything?'

'It was one of Kiriakos' secretaries. Yes, he said that I was being sent to take up a post in Sydney—that's in Australia,' he added helpfully.

'Thank you,' Genista said drily. 'I do know where it is.'

He chuckled. 'Sorry. Anyway, he told me that I'd be flying out there the day after tomorrow. Will I be able to see you before then, do you think? The secretary type said you would be extremely busy, although I don't know how he knew. But I will see you, won't I, Gen? Because I want to thank you properly, and of course to work out how to repay the money I owe you.'

So Marc had kept his word and not told Kevin just how she was going to pay off his debt.

'Certainly I'll see you, but perhaps it would be better if I came to see you at the airport. What time is your flight?'

'Eleven-thirty on Thursday morning at De Gaulle airport.'

'Then I'll meet you at ten. Can you make that?'

'Yes, of course. All right, I'll see you then. Now I'm going to have a bath—I'm sure that bed in the cell had bugs in it!'

Genista laughed again as she replaced the receiver, but she still stood gripping it tightly. Whatever happened in the next five years, however lonely and unhappy she might be, she must always remember this moment; remember that her sacrifice was as nothing compared with what Kevin would have had to go through if she'd left him to his fate.

Resolutely she went back to the drawing-room to say goodnight to her hostess, who herself escorted her to the room she was to use. The room wasn't very large, but it was beautifully decorated and furnished with an antique dressing table and a four-poster bed.

'When Marc telephoned to say that he was bringing you and that you hadn't any luggage, I took the liberty of sending out for a few things for you. I hope you find them to your taste.'

Genista thanked her, and when she had gone crossed to open the boxes and packages on the bed. The first one she opened contained a white lace nightdress and matching negligée that were so fine and gossamer-like that they almost took her breath away. They were the kind of thing you saw in photographs in *Vogue*, but were far too expensive even to contemplate buying yourself. She wouldn't have been human if her feminine mind hadn't thrilled to the thought of owning such lovely things, and she turned eagerly to the other packages to find a set of white silk underwear, some sheer, sheer tights, and a matching fitted dress and coat in a soft, leaf-green woollen material.

Sitting down on the bed, Genista gazed at the clothes, unable for the moment to take in that they were really meant for her. They must have cost a small fortune if the name on the boxes was anything to go by. Probably about six months of her salary, she guessed wryly. Gently she ran her hand over the low-cut nightdress and grimaced slightly at her thought that it was a pity no one would ever see it but herself. But thoughts like that led only to loneliness and she determinedly pushed them aside. There was a small bathroom opening off her room and she found that the maid had already run a bath for her. It felt good to get out of her uniform until she realised with heart-stopping clarity that she would never wear it again. Later she slipped on the lace nightdress and felt its folds caress her bare skin. An ornate, full-length antique mirror stood in one corner and she went to stand in front of it. The whiteness of the garment enhanced the light tan of her skin, gained on a recent stop-over in South Africa, and she had taken down her hair so that now it lay brushed and gleaming dark red on her shoulders against the lace. She would hardly have recognised herself if it hadn't been for her eyes; they stared back at her, wide and green under long dark lashes, but

there was a lost, almost frightened look in them that
betrayed her inner unhappiness.

By five the next afternoon, Genista felt as if she never
wanted to try on another dress as long as she lived. She
had set out with Madame de Frémond as soon as the
couture houses opened the next morning, wearing her
new dress and coat. All the houses seemed to know her
hostess well and as soon as they heard that the clothes
were to be charged to Marc Kiriakos' account they had
almost fallen over themselves to serve her. She found
herself trying on day dresses, and evening dresses that
made her gasp at the price, and was glad to leave most
of the choosing to Madame de Frémond, who had an in-
stinctive flair for what suited her.

They also bought casual clothes; sailing outfits and
beach wear, because her hostess remarked that she would
need them on the island. Genista had been about to ask
what this meant when she had been whisked off again in
Marc's chauffeur-driven car to a shoe shop. And what a
shoe shop! It knocked those in Oxford Street into a
cocked hat. Genista's great weakness was for shoes and
she left the shop feeling terribly guilty and with the
chauffeur laden down with boxes. Her wedding outfit
they bought at Givenchy; a rich, cream dress with a
softly gathered skirt and a little fitted jacket with a half-
collar and big buttons. There was a neat brimmed hat to
go with it, but the bag and gloves they bought elsewhere.
Then on to yet another shop for more underwear. The
amount of clothes Madame de Frémond seemed to think
she needed for her 'immediate requirements' absolutely
staggered Genista, but when she attempted to protest
that she had quite enough already, Madame looked at

her in some surprise and reminded her quietly that as Marc's wife she would have a position to keep up.

This thought was enough to make Genista submissive again, but she was heartily glad when her hostess called a halt and they returned to the apartment. Both her feet and her sense of values were aching badly.

For a long time she lay and soaked in the deep old-fashioned bath before putting her hair up and choosing one of the new dresses to wear. She selected a soft turquoise-blue dress with a layered skirt, a quite low-cut round neckline and short sleeves. Madame de Frémond was waiting for her in the drawing-room and seemed to have thrived on a day that had made Genista feel quite exhausted.

'How charming you look, *chérie*, that dress becomes you. It reminds me of a gown I once wore to a ball in Athens.' She chattered on and seemed in no hurry to go in to dinner, the reason for which became apparent when the door opened and Marc came into the room. He was wearing a dinner suit with a discreetly frilled shirt and black bow tie. In it he seemed even taller and his tanned face more angular. He crossed to greet his aunt and kiss her on both cheeks, then he turned towards Genista.

She found that she had risen nervously to her feet and was annoyed to find that she was shaking. She didn't know how to greet him, what to say, and felt entirely unable to cope with seeing him so unexpectedly. But he, of course, was entirely master of the situation.

'Good evening, Genista.' He took her hand and raised it briefly to his lips, hardly touching it. 'Have you had a satisfactory day?'

She was saved from answering by his aunt, who immediately embarked upon a recital of how they had spent their time. He turned politely to give her his attention, but he wasn't really listening because when Genista stole a look at him she found him watching her with a somewhat sceptical expression on his face. When he saw that she was looking at him, he interrupted his aunt and suggested they go in to dinner at once. 'You will forgive me I know, Tante Mathilde, but I have a great deal to do if I am to have a few days free.'

During the meal he told her that he had arranged for their wedding to take place in the mayor's office of a small town about twenty miles outside Paris. 'The man is known to be discreet,' he informed her, 'so I hope that we will not be annoyed by gossip columnists and photographers. The ceremony will take place on Friday morning, so there won't be too much time for the media to get to hear of it.'

Genista stopped eating and stared down at her plate. Friday morning! But that was only the day after tomorrow. It was too soon! There hadn't been enough time for her to give up one life and plunge headlong into another. She glanced across the table and found Marc looking at her coldly as if he could read her thoughts. She bit her lip and deliberately thought of Kevin who would also be flying away to start a new life. Defiantly she lifted her head and stared back at him. For a second he looked taken aback and then a flicker of amusement crossed his face.

After the meal Madame de Frémond discreetly excused herself and left them alone together in the drawing-room. Genista had crossed to stand by the fireplace while Marc poured himself a brandy. He seemed to take it for granted that she wouldn't want one.

'What have you told your aunt about us? Does she

know that this is—is a marriage of convenience?'

Marc crossed to sit in a chair on the other side of the fireplace, his long legs stretched out in front of the hearth. 'I merely told her that I had decided to marry you and asked her to take you under her wing. I don't find it necessary to explain my personal relationships to outsiders,' he added sardonically.

'I should hardly have considered your aunt to be an outsider,' Genista remarked rather tartly.

'Shouldn't you? But then you're not a Greek.'

This gave Genista pause; she hadn't thought of him as being Greek before, although she supposed that he had rather Hellenic features, but he was much taller than most Greeks and in his dress and manner he was very French. She remembered then how masterful a Grecian man could be, and how they dominated their women-folk. It explained a lot.

He rose languidly and replaced his empty glass on the drinks tray. 'Did Tante Mathilde tell you that we would be going to Akasia?'

'Akasia?'

'It's a small island that I own among the Cyclades group. My father left it to me and I use it whenever I feel like a holiday. As convention decrees that we should have a honeymoon, I decided that we might as well go there.'

'Yes, of course,' she answered in a stilted voice.

Marc looked at her intently for a moment, seemed about to say something, then changed his mind. He looked at his watch. 'I must go. I shall be busy all day tomorrow so shan't see you again before the wedding. If there is anything you need or you have any problems, phone one of my secretaries at the office and he will deal with it for you.'

'Yes. Thank you.'

He reached for her hand again, hesitated for a moment, then shook it quickly before turning to walk briskly from the room.

The snack bar at the airport was already thronged with people and Genista and Kevin had to wait several minutes before they found a table.

'At last!' Kevin said with relief as they sat down. He looked none the worse for his twenty-four hours in a prison cell and seemed positively excited at the thought of going to Australia. 'Why aren't you in your uniform? Though you don't look too bad in that outfit,' he added with brotherly candour.

'Thank you,' Genista said drily, remembering how much it had cost.

He bit into a long, French-bread sandwich thick with fresh ham and lettuce. 'How did you manage to stay on in Paris? I thought you had to get back to London.'

'Circumstances changed. Didn't you have any breakfast this morning?'

'Yes, but it was only croissants, and although I had five, they don't really fill you up at all. What circumstances have changed?' he persisted.

Genista regarded him, her head tilted slightly to one side. Perhaps Marc had been right; she couldn't go on protecting him for ever. He was old enough to know some of the truth, if not all of it. 'Unfortunately the "measly sum" you borrowed was far beyond my means to repay. Strange as it may seem to you, working girls—decent ones, that is—find it rather difficult to accumulate ten thousand pounds, however hard they work,' she told him wryly. 'As Monsieur Kiriakos no longer seems to find your services of benefit to his company, I had no alternative but to take a job in his organisation myself so that I could work off the debt.'

Kevin stared at her, his sandwich forgotten. 'You mean you're going to give up your job? Give up flying?'

'That's about it.'

'But Gen, you can't! You love flying.'

'Would you rather have gone to prison?' She deliberately made her voice hard; this was one lesson Kevin had to learn.

He looked white and shaken. 'Gen, I can't let you do this for me. It's not fair that you should be the one to pay when it's my fault.' He rose hastily to his feet. 'I'll go and see him, tell him I'll. . . .'

Genista gently pulled him back into his chair. 'It's no use, Kevin, there's no other way. If there had been do you think I wouldn't have taken it? If you want to help me, then just please keep out of trouble and try and make a success of this job in Australia.'

'Gen, I can't let you do this for me.' There was a note of despair in his voice and she reached out to cover his hand with hers.

'Yes, you can. Because we only have each other and we have to stick together. If I were in trouble then I'd expect you to do the same for me.'

He gripped her hand tightly with his own. 'I'll save up, every penny I can. Then I'll send you the money so that you can go back to flying.'

She smiled and flicked his cheek with her finger. 'Just keep out of trouble, that's all I ask. Listen, isn't that your flight number they're calling? Come on, I'll walk you to the departure lounge.'

At the door he turned and said her name in a thick, choked voice before hugging her hard and then hastily turning to walk quickly away. Genista crossed to the escalators that carried her up to where she could watch him cross the tarmac and climb up the steps to the plane. She watched it take off safely and diminish to a speck in the distance, but still she gazed up into the sky. She wondered miserably when she would see him again. Probably not for another five years, not until her sentence came to an end.

Madame de Frémond pounced on her the minute she got back to the apartment and she found herself rushed to an exclusive beauticians, there to have her hair restyled into a more sophisticated shape that flicked back from her head when she wore it down. Her nails were manicured, a selection of make-up to suit her skin and colouring picked out for her and packed into a gorgeous leather travelling case.

When they got back to the Rue Fontaine, she found that her belongings had arrived from London, together with a letter from Lyn demanding to know exactly what was going on. Genista thrust it into the bottom of her suitcase; she felt quite unable to cope with anything that reminded her of home at the moment, and spent the evening in helping the maid to pack her trousseau into the set of red leather cases that had also been bought for her. With a flash of independence she also put in some of her own clothes, jeans and shirts; she had an idea that from time to time she would need to look at them just to remind herself of the girl she really was.

It seemed no time at all before she was sitting next to Madame de Frémond the next morning and being driven out of Paris. She looked very slim and elegant, very soignée, in her wedding outfit. Her hair she had put up, and she pulled the hat forward on her head so that it hid her face a little. She felt tense and nervous and kept twisting her gloves in her hands; just like a silly school-girl, she chided herself, and tried to concentrate on what Madame de Frémond was saying.

'Marc has arranged a small reception at a nearby hotel for after the ceremony. There will be just a few guests, close friends and relations.'

Genista wondered how many more times she would hear the words 'Marc has arranged' before the day was out. It angered her that he had told his aunt without bothering to tell her, and it made her even more nervous to think that she would have to face more strangers after the wedding, people who might or might not know the true circumstances of their marriage.

It was market day in the little town and they were delayed slightly as the driver hooted his way through the crowds. Faces peered in at her, some friendly, some just plain curious. The market stalls were piled high with vegetables and fruit, bright yellow grapefruit, golden oranges. Ordinarily Genista would have been avidly interested in the scene, but today all she could think of was the coming ordeal.

Marc was waiting for her in a room at the town hall. He was dressed in a conservative dark lounge suit and there was nothing warm or welcoming in his manner. There were several other people in the room, but he didn't bother to introduce them. Without preamble, he said, 'The Mayor is waiting. We shall go in at once.'

She was led into another, larger room where someone thrust a small bouquet of yellow freesias and white irises into her hand. At one end of the room there was a broad, green-topped desk, on the other side of which stood a short, dumpy man in a shiny black suit with a chain of office round his neck. Marc took her elbow and led her firmly forward to stand in front of the desk, while Madame de Frémond and the other guests found seats behind them. The only indications that this was supposed to be a happy occasion were several vases of flowers around the room and a large bowl of them on the desk itself. Genista wondered fleetingly whether Marc had arranged for those, too.

The ceremony was entirely in French and the Mayor was rather nervous and stuttered so that Genista had to listen hard to understand. Marc stood a little away from her, looking straight ahead. It wasn't until she had to give her responses, say his name, that it hit her fully that she was to be tied to this tall, aloof stranger for the next five years! As he put a wide gold ring on her finger, she looked fully into his face for the first time. His lids were lowered as he concentrated on what he was doing, then he raised them and his eyes met hers. There was something there, deep in his eyes, something she couldn't read, was too inexperienced to define. But then it was her turn to place a heavy ring on his finger. The intimacy of the action with this man she hardly knew and was half afraid of unnerved her and she felt her hand shaking as she slipped the ring on. For a brief moment his hand came over hers, warm and strong. She glanced quickly, hopefully up at him, but his face was set in its usual cold, implacable mask, almost as if he despised her for showing her inward nervousness. Suddenly she was overwhelmingly thankful that this marriage was to be no more than a business relationship.

CHAPTER THREE

THE hundreds of islands, some of them hardly bigger than large rocks, lay below them in the sea like golden nuggets tossed casually down by some giant hand. Genista was seated in the back of the small, luxury jet plane, while Marc sat in the cockpit with the co-pilot, although he himself was in control of the plane. She was glad of this respite to be alone and to rest after the ordeal of the wedding. After the ceremony they had all driven to a nearby hotel where she was introduced to Marc's guests. She had shaken hands with them one by one; a cousin, old friends of his late father's, a godmother. To them all she had given her bright stewardess' smile, and by treating them as she would a plane-load of passengers she had managed to get through the reception credibly enough.

Their drive back to Paris had been a silent one, for she could find nothing to say and was acutely aware of the chauffeur in the front seat, so after a brief glance in her direction, Marc had taken some papers out of his brief-case and studied them for the rest of the journey.

Now the plane banked and began its descent towards a small island that glowed like an emerald-encrusted brooch against the blue of the sea. The clustered white houses of a fishing village came into view for a moment before they landed with only a whisper of tyres and Marc taxied the plane into the shade of a hangar. As they walked towards a waiting car, Genista became aware of the warmth in the atmosphere; it was much hotter here than it had been in Paris, the cool of spring was giving way to the warmth of early summer. Marc didn't bother to wait for their luggage to be unloaded, but drove off straightaway. He seemed eager to get to his house on the island, and Genista could understand why as soon as she saw it. She gave a gasp of delight as her eyes took in the graceful lines of the long, one-storied villa set almost on the shoreline in the curve of a bay. Olive and lemon trees shaded its white-painted walls and everywhere there was a profusion of early flowers, their scents delighting the nostrils as much as their colours delighted the eye.

Marc pulled up in front of a deep, arched porchway and turned off the engine. Turning to Genista, he smiled suddenly, and it was like coming face to face with a complete stranger. 'Welcome to Akasia,' he said with a new lightness in his voice.

A maid showed her into a beautiful bedroom that was furnished entirely in Greek traditional style with a large, carved wooden bed covered with an exquisite hand-made quilt that must have been a family heirloom. Full-length glass doors opened out on to a tiled terrace and there were three wide steps that led one directly down on to the smooth golden sands of the beach. As soon as her luggage arrived Genista changed out of her lovely outfit and put on a dress that was more suitable for the warmer climate. She tidied her hair but left it up; she needed to feel sophisticated to cope with her new situation.

Marc was waiting for her in the large, comfortable living-room and he, too, had changed into more casual clothes; dark blue slacks and a slightly paler blue sports shirt, open at the neck. He had been smoking a cigarette,

but put it out when she came into the room. He rose and
ran his eyes over her, but Genista couldn't tell whether
he approved of her or not.

'It's rather early for dinner yet. Would you like to see
over the house?'

'Please.'

'It isn't very large, although my father extended it to
this size from the original house my grandfather built
here.'

'Does your family go back a long way?' Genista asked
politely.

His mouth twisted slightly. 'Hardly. On my father's
side we are only two generations away from the peasant
fisherman who started off the family fortunes in a
manner that has been kept a close secret ever since, but
which I personally believe was by looting a sunken
Roman treasure ship that he found when fishing,' he told
her with a slightly sardonic smile. 'My grandfather then
went into shipping which led to other interests and made
my own father—although considered one of the *nouveau
riche*—worthy enough to marry into a family of the
French nobility. Which makes me, I suppose, half
peasant, half aristocrat. Which half do you prefer?' he
shot at her.

It was such an unexpected question that she could only
answer stiltedly, 'I hardly know you well enough to say.'

He looked at her for a moment, then said, 'No, I
suppose not. I must remember to ask you again when we
come to the end of your—contract.' He turned away
abruptly and showed her over the rest of the house; the
big country kitchen where strings of onions hung from
the ceiling and where she was introduced to the Greek
cook, the dining-room with its windows overlooking the

hilly centre of the island, and the two spare bedrooms —in one of which Marc's cases stood waiting to be unpacked.

Another door led to the terrace that ran past her bedroom, and Marc took her through this on to the beach.

'Would you like to go for a walk?'

She nodded and he guided her to where a path started off from the beach and led up to a steep rise that ran parallel to the shoreline.

'This leads to a small village called Limani, where the staff who work at the villa live,' he told her.

'Is that the village I saw from the plane?'

'No, that would be Akasia village, which is much larger. It's used as a port and most of the people on the island live there.'

He walked beside her, slowing his pace so that she could keep up with him. There seemed to be a slackening of tension about him, an easing of manner, as if he had thrown off his responsibilities and some of his reserve with his arrival on the island. The track led on beside groves of gnarled old olive trees, but they came to a hollow and Genista drew in a breath of surprised delight as she saw the mellow ruins of an ancient temple. Most of the columns were fallen and broken, but in the centre some had been restored to support a domed cupola. Underneath it, on a low plinth, was a beautifully carved marble statue of a Greek goddess, her right arm raised in supplication, the folds of her gown revealing one naked breast.

'Who is it?' Genista asked interestedly as she walked forward to examine the statue more closely.

'Aphrodite, the goddess of love and fruitfulness. The one the Romans called Venus.' He watched her as she went under the cupola and walked round the statue. 'No one knows when she was first put here, but it was many hundreds of years ago. There's a legend among the people of the island that if a man or a woman loves someone who does not return their affection, they have only to make an offering to Aphrodite and their love will be returned. There is also another legend that if a couple make love here before the temple they will bear a child within a year. But that, I think, is almost inevitable,' he added drily.

Genista turned to look at him quickly, but his expression was completely enigmatical. 'I bet a man thought that one up,' she said rather caustically.

Marc laughed, and again he seemed completely different from the man she had met in Paris only a few short days before. Perhaps being in Greece brought out that side of his nature, just as in Paris he had seemed so very suave and sophisticated.

'Shall we go back now?' he suggested, and almost reluctantly she left the ruined temple to return to the villa.

They sat alone together in the candlelit dining-room, but Genista was filled with a sense of constraint that she couldn't shake off. Possibly it was something about Marc that made her feel like it, for he seemed to be watching her intently, his manner no longer so relaxed. Perhaps he's making sure my table manners are up to standard, she thought sardonically. He refilled her glass with retsina as the maid brought another course, but she hardly noticed what she was eating. He had created a tense, restless atmosphere between them that she couldn't understand.

To try to break it, she said, 'What kind of entertaining do you do?'

Casually he said, 'Mostly dinner parties of from ten couples to about twenty-five.'

Genista stared. 'Twenty-five couples? But that's fifty people! Surely there isn't enough room to seat that many in your penthouse?'

'Certainly not. But I have a chateau near the town where we were married. It's at a convenient distance for people to drive out from Paris. And I also have a house on the outskirts of Athens which I use for entertaining when I'm in Greece.'

'I—I see,' Genista said rather faintly. Once again the enormity of his wealth and position hit her and she sat silently for a few minutes before asking, 'But which is your proper home?'

He shrugged slightly. 'I don't have a permanent base. Home is where I happen to be. It's just more convenient to have a house rather than stay at a hotel in the places where I spend a lot of my time. I suppose, if anywhere, I would choose this place as a home, but I only get time to come here for odd days during the year.'

'That seems a shame.'

He lifted his head to look at her. 'Do I detect a note of pity in your voice?' he asked sarcastically.

'It does sound a rather lonely kind of life,' she admitted.

'Keep your pity.' His voice was suddenly harsh. 'I lead the life I want to live—and I never get lonely. I can have as much companionship as I want, whenever I want it,' he added rather unpleasantly.

'Yes, I suppose you can,' she answered flatly. 'If you'll excuse me, I think I'll go to my room now. It's been rather a tiring day.'

He didn't rise when she got to her feet, but watched

her walk out of the room, his glass twisting in his hand, a brooding expression on his face.

After she had bathed and changed into another new nightdress, this time a white silk one that fastened with just three bows down the front, Genista turned out all the lights except for one small lamp and then opened the curtains again so that she could gaze out at the sea while she brushed her hair. The moon hadn't yet come out and it was quite dark outside, but not dark enough to hide the white tips of the waves as they scudded across the sands and broke on the shore. She pushed the door open a little and leaned on the jamb. It was such a lovely place; she thought that if it were hers she would make sure she spent as much time here as she possibly could.

Behind her she heard a light tap on the door and called out, '*Ela*,' expecting to see the maid, but then the brush froze in her hand as she saw Marc come in and close the door behind him. Slowly she straightened up and turned to face him, her shocked mind registering that he was wearing only a dark-coloured dressing gown over just a pair of pyjama trousers.

In a dazed voice that was scarcely more than a whisper, she said, 'What do you want?'

He raised his eyebrows and answered mockingly, 'I should have thought that was obvious.'

Genista found that her throat had gone suddenly dry and she swallowed nervously. 'But—but you can't mean. . . .'

'But I assure you I do.' He walked over to her and took the brush from her slack hand, drawing her into the room so that he could slide shut the door to the terrace.

He brushed against her as he did so and the contact suddenly seemed to bring life back into her numbed brain. She moved quickly away from him and said fiercely, 'Well, that's where you're wrong! You said yourself this was a business arrangement, and in my book business arrangements don't include going to bed with the boss!'

His lip curled contemptuously. 'Don't be so naïve. Did you really think that I wouldn't consummate the marriage? No, you've been around too much for that, so let's cut out this pretence of injured innocence, shall we?'

She tried to edge towards the door, but he stepped swiftly across and caught her bare arm, swinging her round to face him. 'What's the matter? Aren't I being romantic enough for you? Are you the type who has to have a man tell you he loves you before you'll sleep with him, however little he means it? All right, if that's what you want.' He wound his left hand in her hair and pulled her against him, bending his head to kiss her while his other hand sought the bow at her breast. '*Chérie,*' he began, '*je t'adore.*'

'No!' Genista wrenched herself away from him, utterly revolted. 'I don't want you, do you hear me? My God, do you really think I would have agreed to marry you if I'd known that this was what you intended? Marc, please.' She tried to speak less emotionally, tried to make him understand. 'Look, I'm just someone you hired to help you with your entertaining, that's all. I agreed to marry you just so that I could work to pay back Kevin's debt. Nothing else. I only entered into it because it was to be a marriage in name only. And I mean to keep it that way!'

Marc stared at her across the room, anger in his eyes. 'Do you expect me to believe that? *Mon dieu,* you're either utterly naïve or a damn good actress—and I'm inclined to believe the latter.' He stepped purposefully towards her and Genista backed hastily away until brought up short by the wall. He cupped her chin in his hand and forced her head back so that she had to look at him. 'Do you think I can't see what you're trying to pull? Perhaps you did think I wouldn't want to consummate the marriage and you worked out a nice little scheme for getting money out of me, didn't you? What exactly was the idea? To wait a few weeks and then threaten to cause a scandal by letting the press know, or to sue for an annulment on the grounds of nonconsummation?' His hand slid down to her throat and tightened. 'You're as twisted and rotten as your brother!'

'No, that isn't true!' Genista stared back at him with wide, frightened eyes, appalled that he should think such terrible things of her. 'Oh, Marc, please believe me. I wouldn't do anything like that to you, I swear I wouldn't.' Her eyes swam with tears as she looked pleadingly up at him.

Slowly he loosened his hold and stood a little away from her, his breathing uneven. Some of the fury had gone from his eyes, but they were still cold and hard. 'Whether I believe you or not, I won't risk such a scandal. I would rather you gave yourself to me willingly, but I'll take you by force if I have to,' he threatened her. She still leaned against the wall, her breath coming in frightened little sobs. When she didn't answer he went on, 'All right, I'll give you until tomorrow night to get used to the idea. But don't think I'll change my mind, Genista. When I come to you I won't be denied again.'

The second he had gone, Genista ran to lock the door behind him, but to her consternation found that there was no lock. She stared at the door unbelievingly; she

had never felt so vulnerable in all her life. Slowly, trem-
blingly, she crossed to sit nervously on the edge of the
bed, ready to jump up and put her weight against the
door if she heard him coming back. Then she realised
how futile such a gesture would be; Marc was far
stronger than she and could have pushed her out of the
way easily. No, she would just have to trust that he
would keep his word and leave her alone that night.

Not that he had kept his word about their relationship,
she thought with bitter resentment. All right, he had
never in so many words said that it would be a marriage
in name only, but he had certainly implied it, and he
must have realised that she had accepted him on those
terms. Could he really believe that she had worked out
some dirty little plot to squeeze money out of him? To
take advantage of her situation and his abhorrence of
scandal to blackmail him? Genista grimaced with distaste in the semi-darkness. She supposed that men in his
position must get used to people deceiving them, trying to
trick or flatter them out of their money. It sounded a
rotten way to live; never trusting anyone, wondering
if every person you met liked you for yourself or just
for what they could get out of you. But she felt no pity
for Marc; he'd already said that he lived the way he
wanted to live. Rather she felt an intense anger against
him. Even if he had intended all along to make her his
wife in every sense of the word, then he should have
believed her when she told him that she thought it was
to be only a business relationship. Believed her and re-
spected her wishes, not cheapened her by the insinuations
he had made.

Agitatedly she stood up and began to pace about the
room. But he had made it perfectly clear that he had no

intention of doing anything of the sort. He had said he
would give her until tomorrow night, and she was quite
certain that no pleas or arguments on her part would
make him change his mind. His off-handed assumption
that she would fall in with his wishes made her burn
with resentment. Just because he had women who were
willing, if not eager, to go to bed with him whenever
he wanted, it didn't mean that he could treat her in the
same way. Did he suppose that she was just going to let
him consummate the marriage and then retire happily
into the role he had assigned to her? Did he expect her to
fawn on him, be grateful if he even smiled at her, like
his other women probably did? He might be rich, handsome, and have a reputation among the jet-set for being
an unforgettable lover, but—wedding ceremony or no
wedding ceremony—she wasn't going to sit around and
wait to find out! As far as she was concerned any bargain
there had been between them had been broken by Marc's
actions tonight and she felt fully justified in walking out
on him.

Genista stopped pacing and climbed into bed, sitting
with her back against the hard headboard, her knees
pulled up to her chin. Resolutely she took her mind off
the frightening experience she had gone through and set
about thinking of some method of getting away from the
island just as soon as she could. If she dressed now and
crept out of the house she could walk along the path to
Limani, the fishing village Marc had told her about. But
almost on the thought she foresaw all the difficulties that
course of action might entail. She could hardly ask
some boatman to take her to Mykonos or Naxos, or one
of the other large islands in the group where she could
pick up a ferry, at this time of night. In her imagination

she could already hear all the questions that would be asked—a stranger on a private island with no luggage— for she certainly didn't intend to take with her anything that Marc had provided. Then she remembered that he had mentioned that some of the villa staff lived in the village. Suppose one of them recognised her and sent for Marc! Her flesh crawled as she thought of the punishment he would exact.

No, Limani was out of the question, which left only the other fishing village. And this might be a better bet, because if it was used as a port there would probably be more chance of getting a lift on a boat going to another island. The road from the villa must lead there eventually and she need only follow it and then hang around until first light when she could safely ask for a lift. Her spirits rose a little, only to fall again as she crossed to the window and looked out; dark clouds had obscured the night, there was no moon and she couldn't even see the waves breaking on the shore. She recalled that part of the road they had travelled that afternoon had been cut out of the side of the hill with a sheer drop to the sea below. She shivered as she remembered the sound of the surf breaking on the rocks; then it had merely looked dramatic, but now ...! If only she had a torch. She crossed noiselessly to the door; there must surely be one somewhere in the house, probably in the kitchen. As quietly as she could she opened the door a little and glanced out—then quickly closed it again. A light was shining across the hall from the open door of Marc's bedroom, effectively blocking all hope of escape.

The sound of voices coming from outside woke Genista from the uneasy sleep she had at last fallen into in the early hours of the morning. For ages she had lain awake, occasionally going to peep out of the door to see if his light was still on, but it seemed that Marc, too, couldn't sleep, because it had still been on after three o'clock, and once she had heard him moving about the room. The voices came again, and when she looked out of the window she saw that a large white motor-yacht had been brought round into the bay. A rather swarthy man of medium height but of powerful build stood on the polished deck and was calling out to someone who stood on the shore. Then she saw Marc come into view and walk across the beach. He was wearing a casual shirt over a pair of shorts. He pushed a dinghy into the water and rowed towards the boat where he climbed a ladder and hauled himself aboard. He was very tanned and moved with the easy grace of a natural athlete. The other man greeted him warmly and they talked together, laughing like old friends, for some time. Then Marc glanced across at the house and Genista drew hastily back, afraid that he might have seen her.

Hopefully she wondered whether he intended to go out on the boat today, in which case she might have an opportunity to get away. But perhaps he might make her go with him to keep an eye on her. Worriedly she went into the bathroom to shower, her mind busily trying to work out what she should do. If she pretended to be unwell he would have to leave her behind, but then he might stay too, or more likely set someone else to watch her. She couldn't see Marc giving up any of his pleasures when he could pay someone else to do his dirty work for him, she thought cynically.

After putting on one of the beach outfits she had bought in Paris; a blue two-piece swimsuit with matching shirt, she combed her hair and put on a little make-up. Rather hesitantly she slid open the door to the terrace, then saw that a table had been laid for breakfast further along. She sat down in one of the chairs and helped herself to coffee from the percolator. A maid came from the kitchen and greeted her with a shy, 'Kaliméra, kyria,' before asking her what she would like to eat.

Genista returned the greeting but refused any food; her stomach was already churned up in knots and she couldn't face even a croissant.

'Why aren't you eating?' Marc's voice behind her made her jump so much that she spilt her coffee. She hadn't heard him cross the beach and his sudden appearance unnerved her. He sat down opposite her, his casually open shirt displaying a smooth, muscular chest.

Feeling about in her bag, Genista found her sunglasses and put them on, hiding behind them.

'I asked you why you weren't eating?' he reminded her.

'I'm not hungry.' She tried to keep her tone even, unemotional, but some of the bitterness she felt must have sounded in her voice.

Marc studied her for a moment and then turned his head to tell the maid to bring him breakfast. 'I've had my boat brought round from the boat-house in Limani. What do you think of her?'

Genista looked across at the sleek lines of the powerful vessel. 'It's beautiful.'

'I called her *Aphrodite*, after the goddess in the temple.'

'Very apt,' she replied tartly, imagining what might have gone on aboard the boat in the past.

'She's recently been fitted with a more powerful engine and I intend trying her out today. Would you like to come along?'

'No, thanks,' Genista answered quickly, too quickly.

He reached out suddenly and took off her sunglasses. She stared back at him out of eyes shadowed by strain and fatigue. 'I don't like sulky women, Genista,' he warned her grimly.

'And I don't like men who don't keep their word,' she fired back at him.

Abruptly she stood up and moved to walk past him, but he caught her wrist and pulled her to stand close to his chair, looking lazily up at her through his dark lashes. 'Why all this fuss about such a little thing? I assure you, you won't be disappointed,' he added, a mocking smile playing at the corners of his mouth.

Genista could only glare at him, too furious for words. He laughed derisively and then let her go. Quickly she escaped to the other end of the terrace. Taking off her shirt, she stretched out on a sun-lounger, face down, trying to give the impression of resigned dejection. She didn't have any set plan in mind, at the moment she only wanted him to think that she was too dispirited to try anything.

He took his time over finishing his breakfast, then she heard him walk across the terra-cotta tiles towards her and felt his shadow on her legs. 'Will you change your mind?' She shook her head dumbly and his voice hardened. 'Very well. I've told the maid to come and sit with you. I should hate you to feel neglected on your honeymoon,' he added sarcastically.

He walked away and Genista watched out of the corner of her eye as he rowed out to the boat again.

Soon it pulled away, its throbbing engines so quiet that one hardly knew the boat had come alive until Marc opened the throttle and sent it surging across the bay and out into the open sea, leaving only a crystal turbulence in its wake. Casually she turned over and sat up a little. The middle-aged maid in her black dress and crisp white apron sat at the now-cleared table. She had a large workbag in front of her and was busily embroidering a dainty, lacelike garment as if she had settled down for the day.

Genista lay back with a sigh of vexation; now what was she going to do? From where the woman was sitting she also had a good view of the hallway of the villa, so Genista knew that there was no hope of slipping through her bedroom and out that way. She supposed that if it came to it she could outrun the woman, but there might be other people about to whom she could give the alarm and they might chase after her in a car and catch her. No, she needed at least a couple of hours' start. She stirred restlessly on the lounger; she had no idea how long Marc would be away and every minute that passed lessened her chances of getting away. Then she remembered the car they had travelled in from the airstrip; if she could only get hold of that!

Putting her hand to her mouth, she yawned elaborately, then stood up languidly. 'I'm going to rest for a while,' she told the maid, adding offhandedly, 'Please see that I'm not disturbed until Kyrios Kiriakos returns.'

The woman nodded and smiled as Genista turned and walked into her room, pulling the curtains across behind her. As quickly as she could she changed out of the swimsuit and put on her own denim jeans and a shirt, stuffing her passport and a change of underwear into a shoulder bag. She didn't have much money on her, but it would have to do until she could get to a large town where she could cash a cheque. Deliberately she took off the wide gold ring Marc had given her and dropped it on the dressing table; she wouldn't be needing it any more. Making as little noise as possible, she went into the bathroom and opened the small window that opened out on to the gardens at the side of the house. She might just make it, if she didn't get well and truly stuck in the attempt! By standing on a stool she was able to slowly wriggle herself through, but it was a very tight fit even for her slight frame. Breathlessly she lowered herself to the ground and then stood listening intently, afraid that someone might have heard her. But all human sounds were quiet, there was only the constant clicking of the crickets in the grass and the songs of the birds in the lemon trees to disturb the peace of the morning. She crept round the house towards the carport where the Renault was parked out of the sun, the keys dangling from the ignition.

She had almost reached it when she froze at the sound of someone whistling. A boy came along the path from the kitchen; he was carrying some garden tools and went over to a patch of tilled ground where he started to weed between some rows of tomato plants. Genista watched him in dismay, knowing that to try to reach the car was impossible when he was so close. Perhaps he might give up and go away soon, she thought hopefully as she crouched down behind a bush to wait. But after half an hour of nerve-racked waiting the boy was still there, still less than half way through his task, and Genista decided that she didn't dare hang around any longer; there was no help for it, she would have to find her way across the island and walk to Akasia.

Turning, she crept back until the wall of the villa hid her from the boy's sight, then ran through the trees in the direction of the village as fast as she could go. It was impossible to keep up the pace, the day was too warm and the ground soon became too rocky to go faster than a quick walk. She followed a path, not much wider than a goat track, that led under pines and prickly oaks, with here and there the glory of a flowering cherry. A few late cyclamen still glowed among the forget-me-nots and speedwell that fringed the path and in the dew-wet hollows there were grape hyacinths and tiny yellow violets. A gurgling stream meandered down the hillside and Genista stopped gratefully to cup her hands and drink the cool, clear water. She had no idea how far she had come, but her watch told her that it was already well past noon. She wondered if she had been missed yet and fervently hoped that the maid had obeyed her and not looked in to check that she was all right.

But there was little point in worrying about that now. The path stretched on uphill and she again began to climb it, travelling more slowly now as her legs began to ache from the unaccustomed exercise. It took her another couple of hours before she reached the brow of the high hill where she sat wearily on a rock while she looked about her. Then she gave a gasp of dismay; the track she had been following had brought her out far short of the village. She could just see the white walls of the houses and the deep blue dome of the church away to her left, and she realised that she had quite a distance to travel over rough, uneven ground before she could reach it.

With characteristic determination she set off again

under the hot sun, but with her goal of Akasia in sight
she was more sure of her direction and made better
progress. As she came nearer to the village she passed
increasing signs of civilisation; several thatched, canvas-
sailed windmills creaked near fields of growing crops, a
team of donkeys, laden with baskets of firewood and
black olives was being led down the slope towards the
village, and a woman, black-clad and veiled like a
Moslem, bent to lift bread from a white beehive oven
that stood under an olive tree. The bleak, ochre hills
gave way to lush green meadows and terraced vine-
yards, and below them the houses that were clustered
round the horseshoe of the harbour. The scene was in-
finitely peaceful. There was a primal purity about the
stark whiteness of the houses, broken only by the dark
green of slender cypress trees and the occasional brightly
painted door or shutter among the honeycomb of houses.

At one end of the harbour two men were painting a
caique while others sat around mending their fishing nets
and gossiping. It looked like a scene taken out of time,
a place where nothing had changed for hundreds of years.
Wearily Genista walked down through the cobbled
streets towards the harbour, the black-shawled old
women who sat in their doorways at their embroidery,
watching her curiously as she passed. There were several
caiques, the graceful sailing boats used by the island
fishermen, tied up at the harbour and she immediately
went across to ask if any were going to one of the larger
islands.

The fishermen shook their heads; it seemed that it was
too late in the day for such a trip. With growing despera-
tion, her eyes going constantly to the road in case Marc
should drive down it, she offered to hire one of the boats

to take her to the nearest large island. There was some argument among the men, but like all Greeks they were very courteous towards strangers and eventually some-one was sent to find a man who had business in Mykonos the next day and who might be willing to take her a day earlier, but he lived at the other end of the village and might be out working in his fields, so it would take a little time to find him.

They looked at her dusty clothes curiously, so Genista made up a story that her boat had broken down in another bay and that she had to get help to repair the engine. As she had imagined, they knew next to nothing about powered boats, so were more than willing to be-lieve her. One suggested that she wait in the shade of a nearby taverna, assuring her that they would fetch her as soon as the man arrived. She had to be content with this, and in fact wasn't sorry to have the opportunity for a long cool drink. If she hadn't been so on edge she might have enjoyed sitting in the old, richly-smelling taverna and looking across the timeless harbour to where the bluest sky in the world met the bluest sea.

It was over two hours before the man came and now the sun had sunk much lower on the horizon. He agreed to take her to Mykonos, but named a high price, ex-pecting her to haggle as everyone invariably did in Greece, but by now she was so overwrought and con-sumed with anxiety, sure that she must have been missed, that she agreed to his price at once. The fisher-man stared at her in surprise, then shrugged and helped her aboard his boat that reeked of fish. Genista sat down in the prow on a coil of rope and gave a great sigh of relief as he hoisted the sail and the fresh sea breeze car-ried her out of Marc's reach at last.

The boat was quite an old one and not as fast as some of the newer caiques, but the wind carried them quickly along until soon the island was only an outline behind them. The sky was beginning to turn the blood-red of sunset and Genista suddenly felt very tired. Settling herself more comfortably against the side of the boat, she relaxed for the first time in days and let herself drift off to sleep.

She was awakened by the throb of a high-powered engine and a distant shout. Sitting up, she looked over the side of the caique, expecting them to have arrived at Mykonos harbour, but there was still open sea round them, although she could see a big island not too far away. With a question on her lips, she turned towards the fisherman, but he was looking back over his shoulder, his arm raised in greeting. Genista twisted to look past him and then stared in horror. A boat with the unmistakable lines of the *Aphrodite* was coming up behind and converging on them fast.

The fisherman went to bring the boat about to wait for the faster vessel, but Genista sprang to her feet and caught his arm. 'No, please don't stop! He mustn't find me.' The man stared at her in amazement and Genista added urgently, '*Parakalo, kyrie*, please let me hide so that he won't find me.' She realised that Marc was almost up to them and ducked down behind some crates, praying that the fisherman wouldn't give her away.

But she should have known better than to even ask him; he was a Greek and would never take a woman's side against a man. The boat came round and within minutes Marc had jumped aboard. He dragged her out from between the crates, his face dark with fury. Desperately she tried to struggle free, but he merely picked her up and carried her to the side where he passed her to the swarthy man she had seen with him earlier. She heard him talking to the fisherman, heard them exchange a jest and a laugh, and then he was back on board the *Aphrodite*. The whole thing had taken less than two minutes.

The other man was behind her, holding her by the arms, when Marc came towards her, his expression so murderous that she thought he was going to hit her, but he merely propelled her roughly down the steps to the cabin and locked the door behind her. Then the boat turned and headed back to Akasia, almost flying along as Marc opened the throttle and they surged through the sea at full speed.

He took the boat straight into the bay below the villa and immediately rowed her ashore in the dinghy. Genista opened her mouth to plead with him, but one look at his face, white with anger, made her voice dry up in her throat. He hauled her out of the dinghy before it was properly ashore and pulled her through the shallows and across the beach, to go up the terrace steps and straight into her room. Once there, he pushed her inside before turning to close the door to the terrace. Genista made a wild plunge for the other door, but he caught her before she had gone more than a few paces. Putting his hand in her hair, he jerked her head back painfully and stared into her face, his eyes dark with unconcealed fury.

'So where were you heading? To the nearest newspaper to sell them your story?' he asked savagely.

'No, I just wanted to get away from you!' Genista tried to pull herself free, but the grip on her hair tightened. She gave a little cry of pain, but he didn't loosen his hold any.

'Do you know what the Greeks do to their women when they disobey them?'

His voice was harsh and threatening, but Genista tried hard not to be frightened. She gazed back at him defiantly. 'You can threaten me as much as you like, but I won't do what you want.'

'No?' His voice was suddenly silky soft and far more intimidating than his anger. He took her wedding ring from his pocket and forced it on her finger for the second time. 'We're married, remember? You belong to me.'

'No! I don't belong to you or any man.'

She struggled desperately, but he said angrily, 'I have every right to do anything I want to you.'

He pulled her to him then and his mouth found hers with raging insistence, claiming possession, his hands pressing her body hard against his own. The brutality of his embrace left her shaking and she raised frightened eyes to stare into his. There was a look behind his eyes that made her heart jolt sickeningly. 'Marc, please don't do this,' she begged in little more than a whisper.

'Why not?' he answered cruelly. 'Why shouldn't you give me what you've probably given to a dozen men already?'

Genista's eyes widened in consternation and she drew herself away from him. 'No! How can you say such a terrible thing? I've—I've never been with a man before.'

He had started to come after her, but her words pulled him up short. For a moment he stared at her incredulously, then a derisive laugh came to his lips. 'Nice try, Genista, but it won't work. Everyone knows the reputation that stewardesses have; they're little better than flying call-girls!'

She looked up at him hopelessly, knowing that nothing

would stop him now. 'Marc, not like this, please.'

His eyes glittered down at her as he said roughly, 'It has to be like this—there's no other way.' Then he bent to pick her up and carried her across to the bed.

He had fallen asleep at last; Genista lay still in the big bed and listened to his even breathing. Slowly she slipped from the bed and groped with trembling fingers for the nightdress that the maid had put out ready for her. Her eyes were on Marc as he lay in a strip of moonlight, the light enhancing his muscular shoulders and broad chest. Even in his sleep there was an autocratic, masterful look to his firm chin and hard mouth, only the long dark lashes giving the slightest hint of softness to his features. Frightened that she would wake him, she quickly pulled the nightdress over her head. It rustled slightly as she crossed to slide open the door to the terrace, but then she was through and had silently closed the door behind her. Her bare feet making no sound, she ran across the terrace and down on to the beach.

She had no definite idea in coming out here, only the need to get away from Marc and the humiliation that she had suffered at his hands. Dropping to her knees in the sand, she gazed across the bay. A full moon shone brilliantly, turning the sea into molten liquid that flamed like quicksilver where the waves broke on the shore. The night was warm, but she folded her arms tightly round herself, as if to protect her from all thoughts of the last few hours.

But terrible memories kept coming back and she felt a great surge of hatred for Marc. But then she remembered, too, that when it was over, when he had realised that she had told him the truth, his manner had changed completely and he had tried to comfort her, but she had torn herself away from him to lie on the edge of the bed, her back towards him. He had tried to talk to her, but she wouldn't listen, so he had laid her on her back and resorted to caressing her, trying to show her what love was, what it could be like. She had lain there under his exploring hands, as rigid and cold as the stone statue in the temple, refusing to relax her hatred of him one iota, until he had become angry and had taken her again, passionately, ruthlessly, without pity or tenderness.

Slowly she got to her feet and began to walk along the water's edge, oblivious of the little waves that wetted her feet and the hem of her nightdress. The thought of having to spend five years with him appalled her, but she knew that it would be useless to try to run away again. He would only come after her and drag her back; she was his possession, wasn't she? To be used when he wanted her and then discarded. That her life could be changed so quickly and so much for the worse made her bitter and resentful.

She ran her hands slowly over her body, feeling no different, but knowing that nothing would ever be the same again. Marc, too, had handled her, had asserted his right to touch her where he chose. Her face flamed as she remembered how his experienced hands had fondled her when she lay rigidly beside him. Then he had been gentle and it had taken every ounce of her resolution not to quiver at his touch, not to moan as his fingers taught her a new awareness of her own body. For one brief, shattering moment she had almost turned to him, some need in her making her want him as much as he had wanted her. Then came the knowledge that this was only desire, not love, and the moment was safely by.

But the emotions he had aroused in her made her
ashamed; she felt dirty and tainted. The sea felt cool and
clean against her ankles and impulsively she turned and
waded further out. The water was still warm from the
day's sun and felt like a blanket that nestled softly
against her skin. A need to cleanse herself by physical
effort became irresistible and she set out to swim across
the bay to where some rocks formed a promontory at
the entrance to the open sea. Genista was an excellent
swimmer, and although hampered by the clinging skirts
of the nightdress, knew that she could reach it easily.

It was when she was well out into the bay, but still
some way from the rocks, that the cramp first hit her. An
agonising pain shot through her thigh, making her
double up and swallow water. Choking and coughing,
she came to the surface and forced herself to keep perfectly still, to float on her back in the hope that the pain
would go away. She tried not to panic, but knew that
she had little chance of getting back to the beach under
her own steam. The tide was going out and she would
just have to pray that it carried her towards the rocks
instead of the open sea.

Another spasm hit her and she sank down, down towards the sloping sea-bed. Something caught in her hair,
reached to encircle her arm; for a harrowing moment
she thought that one of the small octopuses that fre-
quented these waters had got her, and she struggled
wildly in an attempt to shake it off, but then she was
lifted bodily to the surface and found Marc holding her
by the shoulders.

'Keep still! Lie on your back,' he shouted at her. 'If
you struggle I'll knock you senseless!'

Obediently she turned on her back and felt the cramp

gradually ease as he towed her back to the shore with long powerful strokes. He half-carried her through the shallows and then dropped her on to the sand, his chest heaving as he fought to regain his breath.

'Why did you go in the sea?' he demanded.

When she didn't answer he pulled her to her knees and shook her a little. 'Answer me, Genista. Why did you go into the sea? To purge yourself of me?' he asked derisively.

Genista didn't look at him. 'Why don't you go away and leave me alone,' she answered dully.

'Leave you alone to drown in the sea?' he jeered. Suddenly his hand tightened on her shoulder so that his fingers bruised her flesh. '*Mon dieu*, you weren't going to ...?' He forced her head up and his eyes stared into hers. 'You weren't—you weren't trying to kill yourself?'

Slowly she let her eyes run over him as he stood so close beside her. His hair was plastered to his head and water ran in rivulets down his chest to where his pyjama trousers clung wetly to his legs, emphasising the taut muscles of his thighs. A sudden flare of red-hot anger surged through her and she was filled with a need to hurt and humiliate him as he had hurt her. Her voice venomous with hate she spat at him, 'Yes, I was! Do you think I wouldn't rather die than have to spend another night with you?'

CHAPTER FOUR

THEY left the island the next morning and flew back to Paris. Marc was again the aloof stranger, his face hard and implacable. He said goodbye courteously to his servants, but treated Genista almost as if she didn't exist. It was almost as if their brief stay on the island, and its traumatic climax, had never taken place.

She sat in the back of the plane again and tried to engross herself in a magazine, but she kept remembering the look of stunned horror that had appeared on Marc's face when she had let him believe that she had tried to kill herself. And she'd got to him all right! He had flinched as if she'd struck him. For a few moments he had seemed completely shattered by her words; his vanity never before contemplating the fact that a woman could find him physically abhorrent. He had taken her back to the villa then and curtly told the maid to stay with her for the rest of the night.

Marc's Rolls was waiting for them when they got to Le Bourget airport and they drove straight to his chateau at Aujon. Climbing into the car, Genista sat far over in one corner, leaning back tiredly against the seat, her gaze fixed on the scene outside the window. As they were now back in the centre of his business empire, she expected him to start work on some of the papers in his briefcase, but he leaned forward to open the built-in cocktail cabinet.

'Would you like a drink?' His voice was completely flat, expressionless.

Genista glanced at him briefly, not attempting to hide the hatred in her eyes. 'No—thank you.'

His jaw tightened and he poured himself a large whisky before settling back in his seat, the silence between them so solid it was almost tangible.

She hadn't really thought about what the chateau would be like; if anything she was ready to dislike it on sight just because it belonged to Marc. To her it would be just another place where she would have to live out the next five years. The car drove between the twin towers of a stone gatehouse, its massive gates opened to admit them, and up a long, straight carriageway. The chateau was a perfect example of French architecture at its best; the two turrets on either side of the blue-tiled, steeply-sloping roof, set above three storeys of exactly spaced windows with, in the centre, a double-branched stairway leading to the massive arched doorway.

In other circumstances Genista would have been enthralled by the house, but now she felt only apathy, a listless acceptance of her changed circumstances; her hatred for Marc the only strong feeling within her. They pulled up below the steps and Marc got out of the car and waited for her to join him, leaving the chauffeur to open the door for her. They walked up the steps, a wide gap between them. A middle-aged woman in a smart navy dress was waiting for them just inside the arch of the doorway, and came forward as they approached.

'This is Madame Hermant, my housekeeper,' Marc told her, and before she had a chance to greet the woman, added, 'Have my instructions been carried out?'

'Yes, monsieur, everything has been arranged just as you ordered.' As she spoke the housekeeper glanced at Genista with a strange, almost triumphant look in her eyes.

Marc led her across the marble-floored entrance hall and up a large circular staircase, the stone banisters in themselves a work of art. He turned right at the top of the stairs and pushed open one of a pair of double doors, standing aside for her to enter ahead of him. The room was large and airy, furnished with Louis Quinze pieces that looked as if they had been made for the room—and probably had, she thought without cynicism. Marc closed the door, but didn't move forward into the room.

'There's a bedroom and a bathroom adjoining this room,' he told her. 'This suite is for your personal use.' She turned round quickly to look at him and he added caustically, 'You don't have to be afraid—I won't be bothering you again. From now on our relationship will be strictly that of employer/employee. You will have complete freedom of the house and grounds, of course, and the chauffeur will take you whenever you wish to go shopping in Paris. You will act as hostess whenever I entertain and accompany me on social occasions. I shall also expect you to dine with me here when I'm at home. Apart from that your time is your own.' He turned to go and then paused. 'Oh, I shall need your passport.'

'Why?' Genista asked suspiciously.

'For proof of your identity. As my wife you are entitled to become a French citizen, but I presume that as this is a limited arrangement you would prefer to keep your British citizenship?' When she nodded, he went on, 'The relevant authorities will have to be informed so that you can be permitted to live in France.'

For a moment she hesitated, but she had no clear idea of French law on the subject and supposed that he must be right. Opening her bag, she gave him the passport.

When he had gone she turned back into the room and crossed to the window. Her rooms were at the back of the house looking out across formal gardens to a small park. The flower beds were ablaze with colour, and she thought it would be pleasant to walk there, but, even as she watched, dark shadows dulled the brightness of the flowers, the sky clouded over and it began to rain. The bedroom was reached through a communicating door on the left, and was again furnished with antiques and dominated by a large four-poster bed hung with draperies of creamy lace. The bathroom, though, was as modern as the one in Marc's penthouse. She wondered briefly whether he would be spending much time at the chateau, hoping fervently that he wouldn't. The less she saw of Marc Kiriakos the better she would like it!

In answer to a knock on the door of the sitting room, she called '*Entrez*,' and Madame Hermant came in.

'Excuse me, Madame Kiriakos,' the woman said in the same language, 'but Monsieur Kiriakos instructed me to show you over the house.'

Being called Madame Kiriakos for the first time shook her so that she stammered a little as she thanked the woman and followed her on to the landing. The house-keeper led her from room to room, all of them beautiful, each in itself housing a small fortune in antiques. Perhaps the loveliest room, and the one that had received the most attention, was the huge dining-room, its walls hung with apricot silk and adorned with large, ornate rococo mirrors that reflected the polished oval table, to which extra leaves could be added until it expanded the whole length of the room. Glistening, trembling crystal chandeliers hung from the painted plasterwork of the ceiling and there were four arched double windows that looked out on to the gardens.

Madame Hermant's manner was outwardly respectful enough, but she took Genista through the rooms grudgingly, as if she resented having her there. When Genista moved forward to examine a Sèvres vase more closely she happened to glance in one of the mirrors and surprised the housekeeper staring at her with a look of pure malevolence on her face. Madame Hermant covered it quickly, but it left Genista feeling shaken. Why on earth should the woman dislike her so? Could she possibly think that her position was in jeopardy, that Genista wanted to run the house herself?

To put the woman's mind at rest, she immediately turned with a friendly smile and said, 'Thank you for showing me round, madame. Monsieur Kiriakos has told me how efficiently you run the house and how much he relies on you. I, too, will have to rely on you heavily and hope you will give me the benefit of your advice and guidance.'

The older woman looked at her blankly for a second, but then she smiled and her manner became much more pleasant. Almost too pleasant, Genista thought with a sigh as, the tour ended, she went back to her sitting-room.

A maid had already unpacked her cases and she found that her other belongings had also been brought from Marc's aunt's apartment. For a while she amused herself by putting out her photographs of Kevin and her parents on the beautiful inlaid escritoire by the window, putting her books on the shelves in the bureau, and rearranging her clothes in the drawers and wardrobes. There was a new box of headed notepaper in the desk, so she spent an hour writing to Kevin and to Lyn. In her letter to her brother she didn't mention her marriage, instead trying to give the impression that she was enjoying her new job; Kevin was basically extremely kind-hearted and she knew that he would be terribly upset if he found out the truth. To Lyn she wrote mainly to give her address and telephone number and to ask her friend to get in touch with her as soon as she had some time in Paris.

That done, she got up and moved restlessly around the room before again crossing to stare out at the rainswept landscape, drawn to the window like a moth is drawn to the flame. She had no idea whether Marc would be dining at the chateau that evening or not, but she bathed and changed anyway, putting on a simple, full-skirted black dress and brushing her hair until it shone like a halo round her head.

At seven she left her room and went to stand rather hesitantly at the top of the staircase. On the panelled walls of the gallery and the staircase hung a whole series of portraits, ancestors of Marc's on his mother's side, the aristocratic side, she supposed. They were intimidating in their powdered wigs, rich clothes and proud demeanour, and she wondered what the haughty women would think of her, the new mistress of Aujon. Mistress of Aujon! Almost she laughed aloud at the title. Many women might have been envious of her position, but she could think of nothing worse than being married to its master! With a somewhat defiant air she went down the stairway and, just as she reached its foot, Madame Hermant came through the door leading to the kitchen quarters.

'Monsieur Kiriakos is waiting for you in the small

salon, madame,' she informed her.

Genista was relieved to find that they weren't going to eat in the huge dining-hall, although the room she was shown into was imposing enough. Marc was standing by the ornate fireplace, gazing down into the flames of the fire that had been lit to take off the evening chill. He straightened as she entered and told the housekeeper to serve dinner at once. Crossing to the drinks tray, he poured Genista a sherry without bothering to ask if she wanted one.

'Did Madame Hermant show you over the house?'

'Yes, it's very beautiful.' There was a silence, and to break it she asked, 'Has it been in your family for long?'

'Ever since it was built. They lost it for a while during the Revolution, but fortunately it wasn't sacked, and then they managed to get into Napoleon's good books and it was returned to them.'

Silence fell between them again and this time Genista didn't bother to try to break it, but, before it could become oppressive, the servant entered and they sat down to dinner. The table was quite small compared to the giant in the dining-hall, only big enough for about eight people, but seated at each end as they were it didn't make for light conversation, especially with the maid going in and out. Marc made one or two comments about the wine and Genista followed his lead politely, but it was like trying to make small talk with someone who didn't even speak the same language, with as little meaning as lines out of a phrase book.

'Shall we go into the library?' he suggested when the meal was over at last.

When they got there she crossed to sit down while Marc poured himself a brandy and turned to walk towards her, but Genista stopped him. 'Could I have a brandy, please?'

He frowned slightly, but then poured one for her and handed it to her.

'Thank you.' She swirled the brandy in the balloon, watching its thick, creamy glow in the light.

Marc sat down in the chair opposite, the crackling fire between them. Such a cosy domestic scene! she thought with bitter irony. Marc's head was bent as he, too, watched the brandy swirl in the bottom of his glass, the glow from the fire sharply outlining the angles of his cheek and jaw and throwing a deep, slanted shadow from his lowered lashes across the hard line of his cheek. There was a withdrawn, brooding look about him that made his face harsh and forbidding. He raised his eyes suddenly and found her watching him. As their glances locked an electric tension seemed to fill the air until Genista deliberately turned her head and looked away.

Standing up rather abruptly, Marc put his glass down and said, 'I've opened an account for your personal use at my bank and arranged for a monthly allowance to be paid into it for you.' He took a cheque book from his pocket and dropped it on to a nearby table.

'I don't need any money,' Genista said stiltedly.

He raised a derisive eyebrow. 'You're the first woman I've ever heard say so. You can start drawing on the account straight away.'

Genista, too, stood up and said tensely, 'I don't want your money. If I need anything that doesn't go with this—this job, then I'll buy it myself!'

'Don't be a little fool! You're bound to need cash for any small purchases you may make, and for tips and that kind of thing.'

'I'd rather you took it off the amount I owe you so that I can get away from you sooner!' she retorted angrily, bright spots of colour in her cheeks.

Marc took a swift step towards her and she instinctively backed away from him, although her eyes still glared at him defiantly.

He stopped just a pace away from her and stared down menacingly. 'I've promised not to touch you again, Genista, but don't try me too far, or by God you'll regret it! While you bear my name and live under my roof, then I'll provide for everything you need. Now pick up that cheque book!' he commanded savagely.

Her face white and tense, her heart pounding, Genista continued to challenge him, then she slowly lowered her eyes, her shoulders sagging. There was no use in defying him openly, that way would only lead to her own further humiliation, for she had no doubt that he wouldn't hesitate to do what he threatened. No, if she was to defy him at all then it must be in secret and only for her own satisfaction. Without a word, she crossed to the table, picked up the cheque book, then turned and walked out of the room.

To Genista the next two weeks seemed like two months. She saw little of Marc; he had to go to Saudi Arabia for a few days and when he came back to Paris he stayed mainly at his penthouse. On the one or two occasions that he came to the chateau he would politely ask her how she was, she replied, and from then on conversation languished until he excused himself to go to work in his study. It was all very civilised, very polite, but Genista knew that his anger at her rejection of him simmered just below the surface and she would only have to put

a foot wrong to turn him again into the passionately
dominating man he had been on the island. So she trod
her path with care, letting him see always that she found
him loathsome, but not stepping over the line that would
precipitate his open anger.

The weather cleared and she was able to explore the
formal gardens, but she preferred the park, which was
more English in aspect and where she could wander
without feeling that the windows of the chateau were
eyes watching her. Once she asked Madame Hermant for
a basket so that she could gather some flowers to arrange
for the house, but the housekeeper told her stiffly that
the gardener sent up blooms from the greenhouses every
day and that she arranged them herself—but, of course,
if Madame was dissatisfied with the way she did them. . . .
Genista hastily disclaimed, for in fact the flowers were
expertly, if rather traditionally, arranged.

Thinking that a visit to Paris would relieve the boredom, she had the chauffeur drive her to the city where
she called on Marc's aunt, Madame de Frémond, but the
maid told her that Madame had gone to stay with a
friend in Monte Carlo for at least a month. So then
Genista determined to really explore Paris, visiting all the
art galleries, museums, markets, everything. But any
pleasure she would have obtained was completely spoiled
when the chauffeur, Morent, insisted on accompanying
her everywhere she went. He was a Frenchman from
Marseilles, stocky but not very tall, a scar across his
cheek giving him a rather sinister appearance. Genista
told him that she would be quite all right alone, but he
persisted in following her, saying that Marc had given
him instructions to do so. So whenever she went to a
museum he trailed behind her, looking bored to death,

and if she went to a shop he would wait by the door, his very presence an irritant that made her return to the chateau sooner than she intended, anything rather than have him follow her all the time. When she wanted to take a car out to go for a drive by herself, they wouldn't let her—Marc's orders again—and soon she realised that she was in fact a prisoner—even if the prison was one of the most beautiful and luxurious in Europe!

At the end of a fortnight, Marc's secretary called her and told her that Marc wanted her to arrange a dinner party for thirty people in two days' time. Genista received the instructions eagerly, even dismissing the arbitrary way they had been delivered because she was so glad of something to do. She spent a couple of hours engrossed in carefully working out a menu with the wines to accompany it and then rang for the house-keeper.

Genista smiled as the woman came into her sitting-room and said, 'Monsieur Kiriakos wishes to give a dinner party on Thursday for thirty guests. Perhaps you will look at this menu I've worked out and then pass it on to the chef. I'll let you know the seating arrangements later.'

Madame Hermant took the paper she held out, but hardly glanced at it before she replied, 'Certainly, madame, if you wish, but Monsieur Kiriakos told me about the dinner-party some days ago and the chef has already purchased what he needs. He could hardly be expected to prepare everything in two days. And as for the seating plan, Monsieur's secretary always sends that to me on the morning of the party. So if you'll excuse me, madame, you'll understand that I have a great deal to do.' The woman looked at Genista, her manner outwardly civil, but again with a gleam of malevolent triumph in her eyes.

'Very well, you may go,' Genista said stiltedly, and stood still until the other woman had gone, then she turned to press her forehead against the cool of the window pane, crushed by disappointment and loneliness.

On the Thursday afternoon she went into Paris to have her hair done, the chauffeur waiting in the reception area. She had it put up, severe on one side, but with soft curls clustering to her nape on the other. Her dress was a swathed sheath of apricot silk jersey, cut low at the back, from the Givenchy collection. She took her time dressing; what was the hurry? There was nothing she had to do, no part to play except to smile and be pleasant to Marc's guests. At seven-fifteen precisely she went downstairs and across to Marc's study, not even bothering to look in the dining-hall on the way to check that everything was as it should be.

Marc was seated at his desk, but he rose when she walked in. He stood silently looking at her, his expression unreadable, until Genista said impatiently, 'Well? Am I suitably costumed to play the part of Madame Kiriakos? After all, it is a leading role,' she added sarcastically.

He continued to study her for a moment longer, then, 'You look—very sophisticated. But there's something missing.' Crossing to a small picture on the wall, he touched a hidden spring that revealed a wall safe behind the painting. He opened it and brought a black jeweller's box over to the desk, sitting casually on the edge. Inside there was a set of emerald and diamond jewellery that made Genista open her mouth in surprise and admiration at their richness and beauty. 'I think the earrings, the bracelet, and yes, the ring as well.'

He held them out to her, but Genista drew back. 'But I can't possibly wear those!'

'Why not?'

'Because they must be worth a fortune, that's why not!'

'They're worth nothing if they're just locked away in a safe all the time. They are meant to be worn; handed down by the women in my family for my wife. It would look very odd if you were the only woman in the room not wearing a single piece of jewellery.'

So it was just a part of the costume. Marc reached out and clasped the bracelet round her wrist, then put the ring on her right hand. It made her remember how he had so furiously replaced her wedding ring after she had run away, before he had.... Her hand started to shake and Marc glanced quickly up at her. Biting her lip, she quickly pulled her hand away. 'I can manage the earrings by myself.' She put them on with trembling fingers while he put the rest of the set back in the safe.

'We'd better go into the drawing-room; the first of the guests should be arriving soon,' he said coldly when she was ready.

So it was an even bigger shock to Genista when the guests started to arrive and he changed in two seconds from an aloof stranger to an attentive bridegroom. His left arm slipped round her waist as he drew her forward to meet the first couple. 'This is Sir John and Lady Marshall, darling.' Others arrived and it was, 'Hello, Marcel, meet my beautiful bride,' or 'Dearest, I'd like you to meet....'

At first she was almost stunned by his performance until his fingers tightening warningly on her waist brought her back to reality and she was able to greet the guests, her smile fixed on her face. Later there was a slight gap between arrivals and she turned to him, her eyes glittering with contempt. 'My God, you phoney!'

He smiled down at her charmingly, his voice menacing. 'Be careful, Genista, someone might hear you.'

'Do you think I care?' Her voice rose a little.

'We made a bargain, remember?' His fingers dug into her waist.

'Which you didn't keep!' she shot back at him.

He drew her closer to his side, his arm imprisoning her. 'Fight me all you want in private, Genista, but in public you're my loving bride.' His eyes glinted mockingly. 'And I, of course, adore you.' And to Genista's furious indignation he bent his head to kiss her bare shoulder.

Dinner was nearly over and Genista was glad that she was seated far away from Marc, who was at the other end of the long table.

'Marc kept you very quiet,' an extremely glamorous American woman seated near her remarked. 'Where did you meet him?'

'We met through my brother,' Genista replied clearly. 'He was a—a business associate of Marc's.'

It was only one of many similar questions that she had parried that evening. Everyone was very curious about her, wondering who this unknown girl was who had hooked one of Europe's most eligible bachelors. However, their curiosity more or less satisfied, Genista noticed that the guests had become bored, especially the women. The men, of course, had their business interests in common and it was purely to further these, or to keep in with Marc, that they had come along, their wives in tow. The women's boredom became even more noticeable after they had retired to the drawing-room, leaving the men to their wheeling and dealing. Almost automatically they gathered into set groups formed by a common language and desultorily exchanged clichés. It seemed that many had already met once or twice that week, for they moved in a set circle of dinners, cocktail parties, night-clubs, etcetera.

One or two seemed genuine enough, especially the younger ones, and were kind enough to compliment her on the dinner-party, but Genista knew that many things had been wrong. They had only been little things: the floral table decorations were too high so that people had to look round them, the dessert was too heavy for the main course, an elderly Greek lady was placed between two men whom she couldn't understand—but put together they added up to a party that had succeeded almost despite the hostess.

Soon after the men rejoined them, their business talk over, the party began to break up. Marc was again by her side as they said their goodbyes, his hand resting negligently on her shoulder this time, but as soon as the last person had left he dropped his hand immediately and his manner became detached and impersonal again.

'That went off well enough. I hope you didn't find them too intimidating?'

'Not at all. The *guests* were very pleasant.'

He stared at her coldly for a moment but refused to be drawn. 'You'd better go to bed. I expect you're tired. Madame Hermant will see to everything. Give the jewellery to your maid and have her bring it to my study.' Then he turned on his heel and left her standing alone.

CHAPTER FIVE

THE following week Genista was delighted to receive a phone call from Lyn.

'I've wangled a four-hour stopover at De Gaulle airport,' her friend told her. 'How about coming out here?'

'I'm on my way. Meet me in the restaurant and I'll buy you lunch.'

'Hark at the big spender! See you later.'

Genista sent for the car to take her into Paris, but she had no intention of having the chauffeur around while she talked to Lyn, so she directed him to take her to her usual hairdressing salon. Here he settled himself in the reception area as usual while she went through the door into the salon, but instead of going through to the cubicles, she slipped into the ladies' room. Luckily it was empty, so there was no one to see her go through another door to a room where towels were being dried off and then out into a yard at the back of the building. From here it was just a short walk down an alleyway back to the main boulevard where she soon picked up a cruising taxi.

Lyn was on the lookout for her and waved as she entered the restaurant. The two girls hugged each other warmly and as Genista gazed at Lyn she felt tears pricking the back of her eyes. It seemed so long since she had seen a friendly face.

'Hey, you look terrific!' Lyn exclaimed admiringly. 'What a gorgeous outfit!'

Genista flushed. She was wearing a soft woollen, hooded blouson two-piece in a rich camel colour that breathed Cardin in every line. 'Oh, it just goes with the job,' she said in some embarrassment.

Lyn raised her eyebrows. 'Some uniform!' Then she looked searchingly at her friend and asked shrewdly, 'What's the matter, Gen? You're not happy, are you?'

Genista looked down at her hands, finding a sudden interest in her manicured nails. 'Of course I am,' she lied. 'It's a fantastic job. I've met loads of interesting people already.'

The waitress came and they gave their order before Lyn leaned forward and said, 'Look, Gen, this is your Aunty Lyn you're talking to, and I just happen to know when you're lying through your teeth. Now you'd better tell me everything, including why you walked out on Paul when you were really starting to have something going between you, and why,' she added drily as Genista raised her left hand to push her hair back, 'you're wearing a wedding ring. Or are you going to tell me that that goes with the job too?'

'Well, yes, you see in a way it does,' Genista answered slowly, and then the whole story came pouring out— Kevin's stupidity, Marc's ultimatum, her marriage— everything except the night on Akasia when he had taken her so violently; that was still too raw and humiliating an experience to talk about, even to Lyn.

When she had finished Lyn could only sit back in her seat and stare at her. 'But—but that's crazy,' she said at last. 'Gen, he must have had some other reason to make you marry him beside that?'

'No,' Genista shook her head. 'I think it's mostly because he hates publicity. The gossip columnists were always linking his name with some woman or other, so he married me to get them off his back as much as anything. Them, and the women he doesn't want.'

'What about the women he does want?' Lyn asked tartly.

Genista shrugged. 'That's nothing to do with me. He made that very clear.'

'And you've got to put up with a set-up like that for five years?'

'I don't have any choice, do I?' She was silent for a few moments before saying with difficulty, 'Lyn, how is—how is Paul?'

Lyn picked up a fork and began to trace patterns on the tablecloth. 'Well, he was pretty shattered, of course, when you suddenly took off for gay Paree, especially when you didn't write or let him know where he could get in touch with you. He kept plaguing me for your address, but I figured that if you wanted him to know you would have told him. So, purely on the rebound, because he was bitter about you, he asked another stewardess to go out with him.' Lyn's voice slowed. 'This girl—well, she'd been pretty crazy about Paul for some time, but with you around hadn't stood a chance, of course. So, even if it meant being second best, a poor replacement in Paul's eyes for the real thing, she did eventually go out with him.'

'But how do you know that ...?' Genista stopped and stared across the table. Lyn was still looking fixedly at the tablecloth. 'Oh, Lyn, it was you, wasn't it?'

Lyn nodded. 'I didn't know what to do, whether or not you wanted to go on seeing him, but when you didn't contact him—well,' she shrugged defensively, 'I knew that if it wasn't me it would be someone else. And Gen, I so wanted it to be me.'

Genista reached across and covered Lyn's hand with her own. 'I'm very glad. I hope things work out for you, Lyn, I really do.'

They stayed talking together until it was time for Lyn to go back to work and then Genista returned to the hairdressers by the same route, pulling her hood up over her head to disguise the fact that her hair looked exactly the same as it did when she went in. The chauffeur was still sitting where she had left him and seemed completely unsuspicious. Genista hugged the knowledge to herself on the way back; at last she had a way of escaping to be alone for a few hours. It was a small act of defiance, just as having her savings transferred to a French bank so that she wouldn't have to use the allowance Marc gave her was another.

Several invitations had arrived at the house and Marc's secretary told her which ones Marc was free to accept. Most of them were from business associates, but a few were from his friends. The former were easy enough for her to handle as they were mostly return invitations from their own dinner-party, but she found her confidence disappearing fast at the thought of meeting people who knew him well. Their relationship was so false that she was sure his friends would see through it at once.

'Not worried about this evening, are you?' Marc asked, noticing that Genista was unconsciously twisting her ring round and round her finger as they drove out to the first of these occasions.

'I'm not looking forward to it,' she admitted shortly.

'Why not? You managed perfectly well when we went out before.'

'They were only your business acquaintances, people who don't know you very well. But you said that these people we're going to meet tonight are some of your oldest friends, they must know that you ... well, that you didn't marry me for....' She stopped, her face hot in the dark of the car.

'For love?' His voice was grim as he said, 'You don't have to worry. They think I've kept you in the background because I didn't want any publicity to spoil our—courtship, and they'll be pleased to accept you for my sake, if not for your own.'

And Marc was right; his friends greeted her warmly, drawing her into their circle. There was much ribbing from the men about Marc, the confirmed bachelor of their set, having succumbed to matrimony at last, and Genista seethed as she watched the hypocritical way he took it, laughing and smiling as if it was all true, accepting their congratulations and coming to take her hand and carry it to his lips, his eyes looking challengingly up into hers when the others drank a toast to their future happiness.

It was a beautifully warm afternoon as Genista strolled down through the formal gardens and descended the steps into the landscaped park. Bees buzzed languidly among the first of the roses and nestlings tested their voices in the still air. Marc had gone to Athens three days ago and she had felt stifled in the house, so she had brought a book out to read in the garden. A kind of bower had long ago been fashioned in the shade of a mass of rhododendron and azalea bushes, their flowers a rich, vivid riot of colour that dazzled the eyes. Genista sat on the stone bench and started to read, but after a while she heard the drone of a plane heading west and looked up to watch it leave a white skytrail against the perfect cloudless blue of the sky. The book slipped from her fingers forgotten as her thoughts went flooding back to Paul. She knew that she should be glad he was going out with Lyn, but she'd liked him so much, he'd been such a wonderful companion, gay and amusing, seldom serious, except when he had kissed her—he'd been serious enough then, she remembered wistfully.

Thinking of what might have been inevitably led her to think of what was, of the cold, strained relationship between her and Marc. Genista thought that she could probably have tolerated the situation more easily if he was always the same towards her, but his abrupt change from cool, contemptuous employer to loving, attentive husband whenever they were among other people made her seethe with inner fury. He was such a sham, made such a parody of the truth. And the worst part was that she had to play along with it, had to smile back with hate in her eyes, had to let her hand stay in his when he held it—albeit clenched in a tight ball—had to stand still when he kissed her ear or her neck although her flesh cringed at his touch. It would all have been so different with Paul; he would never have taken her against her will, never forced her to....

'Genista.'

She whirled round at the sound of a man's voice and found Marc standing a short distance away. 'You!' She let all the revulsion she felt for him show in her face and her voice.

His jaw tightened and he came slowly to stand by her side. 'Who were you expecting?' he asked with a derisive sneer.

Genista bit her lip. 'No one. I was just enjoying being alone.'

He eyed her speculatively for a moment, then seemed to accept her explanation. 'I'm sorry to disturb your solitude,' he remarked drily. 'I came to tell you that some business friends of mine will be visiting Paris next week with their wives. I've invited them here for dinner next Wednesday.' He waited for her to make some comment, but when she didn't he turned to walk away.

But he had taken only a few steps when Genista called after him. 'Marc.' He stopped and turned round, waiting. 'Marc, this dinner-party. Would you let me arrange it myself?'

He raised his eyebrows. 'Of course. That's the whole point of your being here. You arranged the last one, didn't you?' he asked, with a note of impatience in his voice.

Confusedly Genista stared up at him, her mind in a whirl. Then slowly she realised that Madame Hermant must have lied to her. She remembered the things that had been so obviously wrong and wondered if the housekeeper had arranged them deliberately to discredit her in Marc's eyes.

'Well, didn't you?' There was a more searching note in Marc's voice.

Her eyes dropped before his; she had no intention of telling Marc, she would have to deal with this herself.

'I'd like to do something completely different this time,' she said, neatly avoiding the question.

'If that's what you wish,' he said with a shrug. 'But why do you think it necessary?'

'Because last time the guests were bored stiff, especially the women. They'd been to exactly the same party a thousand times before, exchanged the same small-talk with the same polite smiles and assumed interest in other people's lives a thousand times before. Okay, so maybe there was good food and a beautiful setting, but it certainly didn't make for a hilarious, unforgettable evening!'

'And you think you could provide an unforgettable evening?'

'I could try.'

'Then go ahead. I think you might be quite good at it.' And he had turned and walked back towards the house before the *double entendre* of that remark hit her.

Genista knew exactly what she wanted to do and set about arranging it firmly and resolutely. There was, of course, the expected confrontation with Madame Hermant, but Genista had been polite but quite definite in her assumption of authority. The housekeeper had tried to beat her down by pointing out her certain failure, the fool she would make of herself, but, in the face of Genista's determination, had finally washed her hands of the whole thing, refusing to have any part in it. But Genista had found this more of a help than a hindrance. She had gone down to the luxury kitchens to interview the chef and had found him more than co-operative after she had explained her ideas to him, going so far as to make several helpful suggestions. She had then spent a great deal of time on the phone, followed up by visits to several shops in Paris to make sure that everything went just as she had planned.

By Wednesday evening the dining-hall of the chateau had been transformed; the façade hidden by potted palm trees and giant ferns hired from a nursery, the table removed and a Hawaiian band in its place. As the guests arrived they were greeted by smiling, grass-skirted native girls who placed a floral lei around their necks. The windows had been thrown open and they ate an al fresco meal on the terrace, the menu consisting of a wide variety of dishes native to the South Pacific and served by native girls. The drinks had exotic names like Polynesian Punch and Jungle Juice, and tasted just as intoxicating. While they ate they were entertained by the band with their wooden drums and guitars, and later they moved on to the lawn where they were joined by the dancers who demonstrated the hula and other traditional dances. Before long most of the guests were joining in, their exclamations of pleased surprise at the unexpectedness of the party turning to laughter as they started to let their hair down.

'*Mon dieu*!' Genista found Marc beside her as she stood at the edge of the terrace watching the dancers on the lawn below. 'Do you see the so staid Signora Venconzi?' He indicated a rather plump lady in a tight dress who was hulaing with great gusto. 'I had no idea she could be so . . .' he sought for a word, 'uninhibited.'

There was genuine amusement in his voice and Genista realised disconcertingly that it was the first time she had ever heard it. She had heard him laugh before, of course, but then it had all been part of the big act he put on for other people's benefit. She looked up at him, standing so tall and immaculate beside her in the semi-darkness, and found that he was smiling with enjoyment. He must have felt her watching him, for he turned to look down at her. The laughter was still in his grey eyes, but as they met hers the laughter died and his face became an expressionless mask. Someone came up to them and he put his arm round her, low on her waist, his hand drawing her towards him.

Genista shivered with repulsion and he said with

hypocritical solicitude, 'Not cold, are you, *chérie*? Shall I send for a stole or something?'

His eyes met hers with mocking disdain, and suddenly the satisfaction she had gained from organising the evening was turned to ashes and she only longed for it to be over.

But however much the party had turned sour for Genista, the guests pronounced it a great success. She received a flood of calls the next day, not only from the guests thanking her for such a diverting evening, but also from the gossip columns of several newspapers who had already heard about it and wanted more details. Genista tried to squash these, playing the party down and refusing to answer questions despite their persistence.

But her hopes that she had put them off were dashed when she saw the evening newspaper; the columnist had devoted several inches to the party and ended by wondering if Marc Kiriakos' mystery bride was going to bring a breath of freshness and vitality to the Paris scene. Knowing how Marc shunned publicity, she could only hope that he wouldn't see it, but he was home to dinner that night and almost his first remark after they had sat down at the table was, 'I see your Hawaiian evening has attracted the attention of the newspaper hounds.'

'I'm sorry,' Genista answered stiffly.

'There's no need to be,' he replied unexpectedly. 'It was bound to happen. They always seize on anything at all out of the ordinary. Our marriage was reported—with all the usual speculation—the day after it took place,' he added drily.

Genista wondered just what the 'usual speculation' had been, but Marc was speaking again.

'The party seems to have been a great success; my sales

department in the shipping company tells me that they have received an extremely large order that I had quite given up. From Signor Venconzi,' he added with a quirk to his lips. 'It seems that he, at least, had a memorable evening!'

Genista remembered the Signora's impassioned hula. She looked up and caught Marc's eyes—and suddenly found they were both laughing. She stopped abruptly and stared across the table at him, perturbed that they should find anything to share, even laughter—especially laughter. 'I have a headache. I think I'll go up to my room.' She stood up and went to walk out of the salon, her meal untasted, but Marc moved more swiftly and barred her way.

'What's the matter, Genista?' he asked sarcastically. 'Did you suddenly realise that there could be more to marriage with me than this wall of hatred you've built round yourself?'

'I told you, I have a headache. Please let me pass.'

'Not until you've heard me out. For a moment the barrier came down then and you behaved naturally for the first time since we came to Paris, the first time you stopped acting like the victim of some tragedy and behaved....'

'Acting!' Genista broke in vehemently. 'How dare you accuse me of that when all the time you play the phoniest part of all: pretending that this—this travesty of a marriage is the real thing. Holding me, kissing me, giving everyone the impression that we're crazy about one another. God, how they'd laugh if they knew the truth, knew that I found the great Marc Kiriakos absolutely repulsive!'

Marc stared at her, taut-lipped, then, harshly, 'No,

Genista, what they would find really funny would be that Marc Kiriakos had married a frigid wife!'

Genista glared at him balefully. 'How dare you say that? Was I supposed to like what you did to me?'

'Why not?' he asked softly. 'Other women do.'

'But perhaps other women don't get cheated into it by a dirty trick,' Genista retorted, adding malevolently, 'And anyway, I'm not one of your—your penthouse popsies!'

And she had the satisfaction of seeing a completely stunned look come to his face before she pushed past him and went quickly up the stairs to her room.

The spring warmth of June passed into the more humid heat of July and with the summer season more visitors arrived in Paris who had to be entertained. They gave one or two smaller parties which again were written up in the gossip columns, but the *pièce de résistance* was a big party that Genista arranged for Bastille Day. Marc had given her a completely free hand and she had decided to give a *bal de tête* party, where the guests wore their ordinary clothes but their head had to represent a famous person. The invitations, specially designed in the silhouette shape of a head, were sent, although Marc had warned her to expect several refusals as there would be many other parties being given that day. So she was overwhelmed to find that not only had the invitations all been accepted, but other friends and associates of Marc's also wanted invitations, until at last she just had to draw the line because of lack of space.

The party became a guaranteed success almost with the first arrivals, for everyone broke into laughter at the sight of an elegantly dinner-jacketed man, his head a perfect portrayal of Mickey Mouse. With the Revolution in mind, there were several Marie Antoinettes and Napoleons, but mostly the guests showed great originality, and a society photographer was doing great business with his camera. Genista had been a little worried about what disguise to wear herself as she didn't want to duplicate anybody else, but then Marc had suggested she go as Columbine. She supposed she ought to have guessed, but it still came as a shock when Marc came as Harlequin.

The big ballroom on the first floor had been opened up for the occasion and decorated with flowers, its long mirrors reflecting the elegantly dressed dancers and their odd, sometimes grotesque heads. Genista was kept on her feet as she performed all the duty dances, but towards the end of the evening she was dancing with a rather burly Italian gentleman with the head of Charlie Chaplin when someone cut in and she found herself in Marc's arms, his dark eyes glinting down at her through the slits in his black mask.

Immediately she stopped dancing and tried to free herself, but he said softly, 'No, don't run away. Just dance.'

She must have been more tired than she knew, for even as she stood gazing up at him he had pulled her gently back into his arms and was taking her slowly round the floor, the vocalist singing an insinuating love song in the background. Genista could feel the muscles of his arm hard under her hand. He smelt of expensive after-shave, a masculine, woody smell. She became aware suddenly, for the first time, of his attractiveness as a man, a strange mixture of elegant, devastatingly charming Frenchman and earthily passionate, autocratic Greek. He pulled her closer to him to avoid another couple and when he continued to hold her there, his body hard against her own, she didn't draw away, letting him hold her like it until the dance ended.

'Genista....' He started to say something, his voice sounding odd, but just then someone came up to say goodnight and she was kept busy then until she tumbled into bed at last, just as the dawn broke in the sky.

It was nearly noon before she awoke, so she didn't bother with breakfast, going straight to the shower to try to get rid of the heavy-headed, rather listless feeling that she had woken with. The day promised to be hot, so she put on a cool white denim dress and decided to go for a walk in the garden before lunch to try to clear her head.

Marc's secretary was just coming out of his study as she passed and he turned to greet her with a smile. '*Bonjour, madame.* Everyone seemed to enjoy your party. I took several phone calls at the office this morning and they were all highly complimentary.'

Genista returned the smile and thanked him and would have walked on, but Marc's voice called her back. The secretary held the door for her as she went into Marc's study where he was seated at his beautiful antique desk. He stood up as she entered, his eyes running over her slim figure in the white dress and her shining titian hair flicked back to frame her face.

As she sat down he came round to lean against the desk and said, 'I have several invitations here we might go through and see which ones we want to accept.'

It was the first time he had consulted her on this sort of thing—usually his secretary just gave her a list—and she didn't quite know how to take it.

'There's one here for a reception at the Elysée Palace

which we must, of course, accept, and one to spend a few days cruising on the yacht of a couple of friends—you've met them—André and Patrice de Leschall. But we can't accept that.'

'Why not?' Genista asked, remembering that she had liked the couple he mentioned.

He raised an eyebrow quizzically. 'We will if you want to, by all means. But I think I should point out that their boat isn't very large and we would have to share a very small cabin.'

'Oh!' Genista flushed hotly.

'Exactly,' Marc said drily.

They sorted through the rest of the invitations; a concert in aid of a charity for sailors, a cocktail party at the Greek embassy, several private dinners, a film premiere, a polo match; it seemed to Genista as if there was something happening every day as she noted the engagements in her diary.

'I think those are the most important,' Marc remarked as he finished going through the pile of cards. 'I'll get my secretary to send letters of apology to the others.'

Genista started to get up from her chair, but Marc put his hand on her shoulder. 'No, don't go. I have something for you.' He went round to the front of his desk and took a slim white box from a drawer. He dropped it casually into her lap as he came to stand near her again. 'That's for all the hard work you put into last night's party,' he told her offhandedly.

Taking her time, Genista slipped the diary into her pocket before picking up the box. Its lid bore the name of a famous Paris jewellers. Slowly she opened it and then her breath caught in her throat. It was a bracelet; a beautiful, beautiful platinum bracelet in an ultramodern design of curled leaves, and in the heart of each leaf, nestling like a drop of morning dew, there lay a sparkling diamond.

When her breath came back at last, Genista said slowly, 'I don't quite understand. You mean that this bracelet is to go with the collection in your safe that I choose from when we got out, don't you?'

Marc shook his head, his eyes watching for her reaction. 'No, I mean that it's for you. A present.'

Genista felt her skin go tight as she looked at the bracelet. 'How much did it cost?' she asked stiltedly.

She felt, more than saw, his eyebrows go up at that. 'That's a question a lady never asks,' he answered with a trace of amusement in his voice.

Her cool green eyes looked up into his. 'To quote a prehistoric cliché: I'm no lady, I'm your wife. But not the kind who accepts expensive presents,' she added, thrusting the box back at him.

Calmly he folded his arms and looked at her somewhat derisively. 'Don't put any hidden meaning into the gift, Genista. It was merely meant as a—shall we call it a bonus? for the originality and effort you put into our party. The cost of the bracelet is nothing to me. I give it to you just as I'd give a tip to a waiter in a restaurant.' His hands came down to grip the edge of the desk. 'What did you think it was?' he asked sarcastically. 'An inducement? Did you think I was trying to bribe you into letting me make love to you again?'

Genista was on her feet now facing him, with two bright spots of colour high on her cheeks, her eyes no longer cool but as fiery as emeralds. '*Love* didn't come into it!' she retorted fiercely.

His lips tightened into a thin line and he stared back

at her angrily, but then he shrugged. 'No, it didn't,' he agreed. 'Nor does it now. So you will take the bracelet and wear it or not, as you please.' He went round to the other side of his desk and sat down. 'Now, if you'll excuse me, I have a great deal of work to do.'

Dismissed, Genista hesitated for only a moment before leaving the study, the jeweller's box still in her hand. She continued on her interrupted way into the garden and strolled unseeingly among the massed flower beds. She felt strangely hurt and humiliated; Marc had set her firmly back in her position as employee, although a favoured one, she thought ironically, remembering the value of the bracelet, and somehow his attitude had hurt. Taking herself to task, she realised that the success of her parties and Marc involving her in going through the invitations must have gone to her head a little. The only thing that had changed was that they were seeing more of each other and she was coming to take for granted the act of loving husband that he played for others. And for a moment, back there in his study, she *had* thought that he wanted her again. Distractedly she picked a piece of yellow laburnum from an overhanging branch and pulled it to shreds as she walked agitatedly along. For a few minutes she had wondered if perhaps the very fact that she hated him acted as a challenge. She was pretty certain that very few women had ever said no to Marc, and the thought that the one woman he had a right to take had refused him could quite possibly goad him into trying to make her fall for him.

But his insistence that the cost of the bracelet meant nothing to him had quickly killed that idea. So why wasn't she relieved? Genista came to a halt and leaned back against the high wall that surrounded the chateau.

She ought to be glad that he didn't want her, glad that their relationship was now purely on a business footing. Gazing down at the ruins of the laburnum, Genista acknowledged her own feelings; now she had something to occupy her, a job that stretched her ingenuity and organising abilities, she found that she was happier than she ever thought she would be in this situation. Her training in handling people of every nationality had paid off, she enjoyed meeting Marc's business friends and was pleased when he mentioned that a deal had come off or a useful contact made.

She knew that it was the kind of life she could thrive on if it had really been just a job. And she had to admit that if she had been just his social secretary, then she would have enjoyed working with Marc, enjoyed going through the pile of invitation cards with him and discussing guest lists, finding out which people were enemies and which were friends and who spoke what languages. As a boss he would have been marvellous; charming and considerate, making her feel feminine by his very masculinity, and the perks—the uniform, as Lyn had called her clothes—were, of course, out of this world. She realised that she could, despite all her first reluctance to take on the job, have been thoroughly enjoying herself now if it hadn't been for Marc's brutal insistence on consummating the marriage. By doing so he had ruined every chance of a happy working relationship. For there was always a kind of tension between them, mainly due to her resentment at his callousness, but there was also a basic sexual awareness of each other as a man and a woman.

Taking the jeweller's case from her pocket, Genista opened it and stared again at the bracelet. Could he, perhaps, have given it to her by way of a peace-offering? Something that he hoped would atone for what he had done when he was too proud to say it himself? Genista shook her head in bewilderment; she had read first evil and then good into the gift, so that now she didn't know what to believe. She sighed and started to walk back to the house, but presently her shoulders straightened; she still had nearly five years in which she would have to tolerate Marc's company, and five years was a long time to go on hating anyone. For whatever reason he had given her the bracelet, all that really mattered was that he was pleased with her work, and if she had to work with him then she might as well get as much enjoyment out of it as she could.

From that point on their relationship altered gradually. When Genista looked at Marc her eyes were no longer filled with dislike, when he touched her she didn't immediately pull away as she had done before, and she began to take more interest in his business, becoming aware of the subtleties of high finance and the usefulness of contacts. As the summer progressed she relaxed more in his company and Genista found herself often laughing spontaneously at some story he told her or witty observation he made. Marc seemed to be able to spend more time at the chateau and very seldom stayed overnight at the penthouse. She began to look forward to the times when they entertained or went out together, though hardly even admitting to herself that she rather liked the possessive way he behaved towards her on these occasions and that her pretence of loving wife wasn't quite such an act after all.

It was at the reception at the Elysée Palace that she first met Sheik Aly Ben Fahid. She and Marc had stood smiling for the usual crowd of magazine photographers and had just passed along the receiving line, when a man in an immaculate dinner suit, his strong, hawklike face deeply tanned under his black curly hair, but with laughing, gentle brown eyes, came up to them.

'So it was true what they told me,' he remarked without preamble, his eyes running over Genista appreciatively. 'Your stone goddess has come to life and turned into a woman of fire to warm that cold heart of yours.'

Genista's eyebrows rose at this flowery language, but Marc merely laughed and greeted the man with a warmth that was unusual in him. 'Aly! *Mon cher ami*. When did you get to Paris? Why didn't you come straight to see me?'

'I didn't want to spoil your happiness, my friend. I knew that once your beautiful bride set eyes on me you would become as nothing in her eyes and she would want only to become my tenth wife.'

Marc grinned and pretended to wave a menacing fist in the other man's face. 'Go back to your harem, Aly, this one's mine.' He put a protective arm round Genista and drew her close to him, his thigh hard against her own, but Genista could only goggle at the Arab.

'Do you really have ten wives?'

'No, only nine at the moment,' he told her without a blink, 'but I will put your name down to be number ten just as soon as we can get rid of this little Frenchman,' he added.

'The "little Frenchman" has knocked you down many times before and will do so again in a moment,' Marc warned, then turned to Genista and said, 'Believe it or not, darling, this reprobate is one of my oldest friends, we went to university together. His name is Sheik Aly

Ben Fahid, Aly to his friends, one of whom I'm sure he will soon make you. But don't let him fool you; he doesn't have any wives, no woman in her right mind would ever take him on.'

'Why not?' Aly asked incorrigibly. 'You finally found one who would tolerate your uncouth bourgeois manners, and a most lovely one at that.' He raised Genista's hand to his lips, his deep brown eyes teasing her when she tried to draw it away and he wouldn't let go. 'No, you must come and talk to me. We will leave the *pauvre petit* Marc to his business affairs while you tell me what you thought you saw in him and why you now regret marrying him, and I will tell you all about the palace I will build for you in my country.' He resolutely pulled her arm through his and led her away.

Genista looked back over her shoulder at Marc, but he merely smiled and raised his hands in a helpless gesture before turning to greet an acquaintance. Aly led her to a seat and demanded that she tell him all about herself.

'Oh, no, you first,' Genista countered with a smile. 'How long have you known Marc, and where is this country of yours?'

He answered her readily enough and Genista soon found that beneath his banter he was a warm and sincere person. She immediately felt at ease with him and, despite all his lurid plans for her future with him instead of Marc, found that she was quite safe with him. He tried to draw her out to tell him about herself, but she laughingly parried his questions. He continued to tease her for a little until he saw that she really didn't want to tell him.

'So I was right, then,' he exclaimed triumphantly. 'You are the statue of Aphrodite in Marc's temple come to life.

A woman without a past.'

She knew that he had drawn his own conclusions, but let it go. If he wanted to know about her then he must ask Marc. Whether Marc would tell him or not would probably depend on how close a friendship there was between the two men, but somehow she couldn't see Marc's pride allowing him to tell anyone the whole truth, just as hers hadn't allowed her to tell Lyn.

When Aly took her back to Marc at last, he said, 'I am going to take Genny out to lunch tomorrow, Marc. We haven't yet decided on exactly how we are going to decorate our bedchamber. I warn you, if you say no, I will fight you for her.'

His expression was so fierce that Genista had to laugh and Marc grinned perfunctorily. 'I'm terrified,' he mocked. Genista expected him to play his usual possessive role, but instead he said, 'Yes, of course have lunch together. Do so whenever you wish.' He spoke almost offhandedly, as if his mind was on something else. Then, 'Look after Genista for a bit longer, would you, Aly? There's someone I really must talk to.' And then he was gone, lost in the crowd of guests.

Genista watched him go, his unusual action making her feel strangely alone for a moment. Then she turned to Aly, her eyes unnaturally bright, and said lightly, 'It seems you've got me sooner than you expected.'

He gave a slight shrug. 'It's the way of the world, Genny—Marc's world.'

There was understanding in his kind eyes and Genista felt an odd empathy between them that was to be the start of a growing friendship. And she found that she needed a friend, someone who made no demands of shared confidences as a woman might, just someone who could make her relax and laugh, and who provided an alternative to being in Marc's disturbing company or being alone at the chateau. After that first lunch he often took her out during the day when Marc was busy, as he seemed to be more than ever now. He took her to parts of Paris she didn't know existed and let her drive his powerful car out into the Normandy countryside to eat at small wayside inns slumbering in the heat of the long summer.

What Marc thought of these expeditions she didn't know, for he said very little, merely enquiring where they had been and whether she had enjoyed herself. He was again away a lot, jetting to different parts of the world, his face preoccupied and a tired look about his eyes. When Genista tried to find out if anything was troubling him he cut her off short, almost snubbing her in his abruptness, so that she didn't ask again. So to Genista her outings with Aly were a welcome relief, a chance to stand aside from her own situation for a while and let the tensions of living a lie ebb away from her. She couldn't understand this sudden change in Marc's attitude to her when they had seemed to be getting on better terms, and having Aly as an escort helped to take her mind off the problem. She didn't know whether Marc had told him the truth and he never again asked her about herself—he was that kind of friend. He was Genista's friend, but he was Marc's too, in that he never made a pass at her, even though he kept up the game of pretending to lure her away from Marc. He dressed well, but unostentatiously, and Genista had thought him only moderately well off, so she was staggered when he mentioned that he had to go to a meeting of OPEC and she found out that he owned, actually owned, one of the richest oil-producing sheikdoms in Arabia!

He was naturally invited to all the parties at the chateau, although some of these had to be cancelled because of Marc's absence, and he became interested in what she was doing to try to brighten up the social round, often making outlandish suggestions. And when he found out how much she hated having the chauffeur follow her everywhere he dismissed the man with a languid wave of his hand and escorted her himself instead.

One morning he came to collect her in his blood-red Ferrari and let her take the wheel until they parked in the centre of Paris. They climbed the many flights of wide stone steps up to Montmartre and sat down at a pavement café in the Place du Tertre where they idly sipped coffee and watched the tourists thronging round the easels of the many artists who made their living by painting, over and over again, the lovely white domed church of the Sacré-Coeur.

It was strange, Genista reflected, both she and Aly were foreigners, but she had always felt at home in France and Aly seemed to blend in with the French people perfectly; perhaps it was because they both spoke French so fluently. The tourists stood out a mile as they tried to make up their minds over the paintings or sat to have their portraits drawn by one of the local artists.

Aly must have guessed her thoughts, for he said suddenly, 'Today we are going to become tourists. We are going to do everything the tourists do.' He called across to one of the artists and asked him to sketch her, but proceeded to make a great nuisance of himself by insisting that she wasn't positioned properly and himself turning her head into exactly the pose he wanted. Then

he stood behind the poor artist and made remarks like :
'No, no, her eyes are larger than that! Can you not see
that they are as green pools and her lashes like the soft
grass round an oasis? And her nose; her nose is perfection
and you have drawn an ordinary, common nose!'

The poor man must have been cursing him, but the
size of the note that was slipped into his hand when he
had finished immediately brought an amazed smile back
to his face again. Genista was gurgling with laughter; she
was used to Aly adopting a flowery turn of speech whenever he put on his 'Sheik of Araby' act, as she called it,
but the people who had gathered around appeared
slightly stunned.

'And now we go to Notre Dame,' he announced. And
go to it they did—right up the stone spiral staircase that
led to the roof of the left-hand tower where the hunch-
back was supposed to have looked down on the crowds
who had gathered to kill the girl he loved.

Afterwards they ate lunch on board one of the *bateaux
mouches* while sailing along the Seine. Aly was talking
away, but Genista found that she was gazing abstractedly
through the window, her mind far away. She had been
greeted at breakfast that morning by Madame Hermant,
who, with scarcely veiled hostility, had informed her
with some relish that Marc had left early that morning
for West Africa and didn't know when he would be
back. For some reason the news had depressed her,
though why it should she didn't know. He had gone
abroad several times before, often only telling her
through his secretary, but somehow the thought that he
had gone away this time without saying goodbye to her
had hurt.

Aly gently touched her hand and she jumped. 'Oh,

I'm sorry, I was miles away. What were you saying?'

'It hasn't helped, has it, *ma mie*? Our playing at tourists? You're still thinking about Marc?'

Genista looked down at the table. 'Was it that obvious?'

'Only to someone who knows you well. Unfortunately you're rather good at hiding your true feelings.'

'Unfortunately?'

'Yes, because I think you have learnt to hide yours through unhappiness. But usually you are natural with me. It is only when you're with Marc that you assume your false face, beautiful though it is,' he added with a smile.

Genista blinked, then said slowly, 'He's been so preoccupied lately, rushing about all over the place and tiring himself out. Aly, do you know what's troubling him?'

'If I did I wouldn't tell you. It's for the husband to tell his wife as much as he wants her to know. In my country you wouldn't dare to ask!' Genista made a face at him and he grinned. 'Not, of course, that I would ever leave your side once I had you installed in that palace next to mine.'

He teased her until he made her laugh, then said more seriously, 'I have a great favour to ask you, *ma petite*. I have to go back to my country for a few weeks, but before I go I wish to give a party for all my friends in Paris. It would give me great pleasure if you would organise it for me.'

'Why, of course I will. I'd love to. For how many people?'

'I thought about three hundred.'

Genista stared and said faintly, 'Where were you

thinking of holding it?'

Aly smiled. 'I've just bought a house near the Boulevard St Germain which has a room big enough. If you have finished, I'll take you to see it.'

The house turned out to be a mansion that must have cost all the profits from a year's supply of oil, with beautiful high-ceilinged rooms and a vast ballroom. 'Do whatever you wish,' he told her. 'Disregard the cost.'

So Genista took him at his word and on the night of the party had transformed the house into a Moorish palace, the ballroom hung with golden draperies to resemble a great tent and with tinkling fountains and ornate mirrors that reflected the softly-glowing lamps and sconces around the walls. The guests had been promised a page out of the Arabian Nights and they had nearly all entered into the spirit of the thing by wearing Arabian costume. There were a great many Caliphs and Grand Viziers, and even more bare-midriffed, veiled slave girls, but Aly outshone them all in a flowing black robe and startlingly white headdress, a bejewelled scimitar at his waist and the hilt of a dagger protruding from the top of his soft black leather boots. He had lent Genista a gown that had belonged to his mother which was also black, but richly embroidered with silver thread. It covered her far more than the slave girls' costumes, but gave her an air of mystery and hidden beauty with its full trousers gathered at the ankles, slit sleeves giving a hint of her bare arms, and the swathing headdress that veiled all but her green eyes.

Genista took care to stay in the background, leaving Aly to greet all the guests; she knew how easily gossip could arise if she wasn't careful, especially as Marc was still away. There had been no word from him and she didn't know when he would be back. Not that she expected him to let her know. Because of her veil, very few people recognised her and she felt strangely reluctant to make herself known, content to stand to one side while they watched a group of dancers performing to Borodin's compelling music from *Prince Igor*, followed by a host of entertainers who wandered about the great rooms performing their acts : jugglers, tumblers, fire-eaters; it created an exotic atmosphere of gaiety and excitement for the jaded Western palates. There were exclamations of wonder at the large platters of strange foods that were spread out on the long tables, shouts of encouragement for the belly dancers and little gasps of horror that changed to laughter when the snake-charmer's dangerous-looking serpent turned out only to be an imitation.

But suddenly Genista found that the edge had gone off the evening; perhaps it was because she had organised it and the novelty had worn off, perhaps it was because she was alone. She found a seat in a corner by one of the fountains in a small side room and sat down rather list-lessly. Despite the enmity that existed between her and Marc, and even though she knew only too well that his attentions towards her were merely an act, she found that she still missed him. Living under the same roof and being so much in one another's company had made her rather take him for granted, but the house seemed even more lonely and empty without his forceful presence and the party dull without him constantly at her side. Aly, of course, had been a wonderful companion, but at the back of her mind she couldn't help wondering if Marc hadn't asked him to take care of her while he was away.

'Now why are you hiding yourself away in here, oh future queen of my harem?' Her reverie was interrupted as Aly strode into the room.

Genista smiled. 'You know, you really shouldn't say things like that because one day I might take you seriously and turn up on your doorstep. Do harems have doorsteps?'

'Of course. With a huge mat with Bienvenue written on it.' He came to sit beside her and took her hand, suddenly serious. 'Genista, I hope you will remember that you will always be welcome in my home. And not necessarily in the harem, although you would be more than welcome there too.'

His eyes were regarding her with sincerity, and with something else deep in their depths. She said huskily, 'Thanks, Aly, but there are times when a girl has to stand on her own two feet.'

'If that's what western civilisation does for women then I shall definitely ban it in my country.' Genista tried to draw her hand away, but he wouldn't let go. Instead he took a ring, a ruby set in antique gold, from his little finger and slipped it on to her hand. 'I want you to take this as a small memento of the happy times we have spent together, *ma petite*. It will give me great happiness if you would sometimes wear it and think of me.' He raised her hand and carried it gently to his lips.

After a moment Genista took her hand away and slowly removed the ring. 'It's very kind of you, and I understand why you want to give it to me, but I can't accept the ring, Aly. I'm sorry.'

'Not even from a friend?'

She shook her head decisively.

He sighed and took the jewel from her outstretched palm.

'But thank you for wanting to give it to me and thank you for being a friend.' Genista leant towards him and kissed him lightly on the cheek before getting to her feet. 'If you don't mind, I think I'll go home now. I'm feeling rather tired.'

He came with her to the door and as the car drew away she turned to wave to him, a magnificent figure framed in the light of the entrance.

Having expected to be late back, Genista had told the servants not to wait up, so she let herself into the house. The portraits looked down at her eerily in the glow of the one light that had been left on for her. She started to go upstairs but then changed her mind; she was tired, but somehow she knew she wouldn't sleep, she felt too restless and fidgety for that. Crossing the hall with its black and white chequered marble floor, she went into the drawing-room and through the french windows on to the terrace. It was a lovely night, the stars glinting like diamonds against the black velvet of the sky and the full moon silvering the white roses that climbed the old walls of the chateau. Reaching up, she picked one of the roses, but gave a little exclamation of pain as she pricked her finger.

'Need some first aid?'

Genista whirled round at the sound and stared at the dark figure that stood in the shadows. 'Marc!'

He stepped forward into the moonlight and strolled across the terrace to sit casually on the balustrade. 'You look as if you're ready to join Aly's harem,' he said tightly as he ran his eyes over her slender figure, the outline of her body through the thin material highlighted by the moon's radiance.

'No, I just escaped from it,' she answered, trying to keep her voice light. She moved closer to him so that she could see his face. 'When did you get back? Have you eaten?'

'Yes, on the plane.' He reached up and undid her veil. 'I'm glad you escaped,' he said with unexpected gentleness. His hand slid to her throat, warm and strong. As his thumb began to slowly stroke her shoulder-blade, Genista began to quiver uncontrollably and then her body became rigid under his hand.

Immediately he took his hand away and stood up. His face was fully in the light of the moon now and she saw that the gentleness was gone and in its place for a moment there was a blend of anger and tiredness overlaid by a strange and alien bitterness, but the tension was gone from his eyes and he seemed relaxed for the first time in weeks.

'It's over, isn't it? This thing you've been working on?'

Marc looked surprised. 'You're very perceptive. Yes, it's over, thank God.' He turned and stood beside her, looking out over the moonlit gardens, and suddenly, inexplicably, Genista felt content.

CHAPTER SIX

MARC never told her what had kept him so busy, but when she read in the newspapers that France had successfully negotiated a complicated trade deal with one of its former colonies which involved the repatriation of several political prisoners, it made her wonder if this had been the cause of his worry and his subsequent trip to Africa. He was busy again now, catching up on the accumulated work at the office, but Genista had cause to be glad he wasn't around when she had an unexpected phone call from her brother telling her he was back in Paris and staying near his old flat. She didn't ask him why he was there over the phone; she was too aware of the possibility of Madame Hermant listening in on one of the extensions, so she merely told him to wait for her and she would come to him. Deciding that it would be better if Marc didn't know he was in Paris, she went through the routine of giving the chauffeur the slip at the hairdressing salon before taking a taxi to Kevin's flat; she didn't know whether the chauffeur reported her activities to Marc, but thought it better not to take the chance.

Once in his room, she hugged Kevin, but then pushed him away to look at him in worried exasperation. 'All right, what have you been up to this time? You didn't get the sack again, did you?' she asked anxiously.

There were lines of tiredness from his long journey round his eyes, but apart from that he looked tanned and fit. 'No, I came back because of you.' He pulled a piece of paper from his pocket and gave it to her.

Slowly Genista unfolded it; it was a page torn from a glossy magazine that specialised in reporting Parisian society. There was a large photograph showing herself and Marc arriving for the reception at the Elysée Palace. The caption underneath made their married status quite clear. Almost detachedly she noted how Marc had his arm round her possessively, the way he was looking down at her with loving pride for the sake of the cameras. Her fingers curled and she screwed the sheet into a tight ball which she dropped into the waste paper basket before turning to meet Kevin's accusing gaze.

'Are you really married to him?'

'Yes, I am,' she replied coolly.

'But, Gen, I don't understand. Did you—did you fall for him or something? And why didn't you let me know?' There was anxiety now in the eyes so like her own.

Genista sighed slightly, knowing that she couldn't protect him any longer. 'I had to marry him, Kevin. It was part of the bargain we made.'

He sat down slowly in a chair. 'You'd better tell me all about it.'

She crossed to stand behind him, putting her hands on his shoulders while she told him. His first reaction was blazing anger at Marc for giving her no alternative, his second bitter self-recrimination for having put her in such a position.

'Oh, Gen, you must hate me for what I did! But why didn't you tell me? I'd have got the money somehow.' He stood up and squared his shoulders. 'But now I'm here I'll go and see him, tell him he's got to set you free. I'd rather go to prison than have you married to someone you don't love.' He looked at her searchingly. 'You don't love him, do you, Gen?'

Slowly she raised her eyes to look into his. 'No, I don't. At first I—I hated him, but now....' She shrugged. 'I suppose I've got used to the idea, and I really quite like all the work involved. And it's not as bad as you think; I stipulated that it would only be for five years. That isn't very long, the time will just fly by.'

He stared at her. 'But you'll be nearly thirty. That's ancient!'

'Thanks very much!' his sister replied tartly, then grinned at his shocked face. 'Look, you're free, that's all that really matters. Now suppose you tell me why you came haring back to France instead of just writing to me?'

Kevin looked somewhat shamefaced. 'When I saw that photograph I just drew out all the money I'd been saving and flew back. I knew you couldn't have married such a cold fish as Kiriakos from choice and I thought you might need me.'

Inwardly Genista smiled at his description of one of Europe's ex-most eligible bachelors, but hastened to reassure him that there was nothing he could do.

'If only I could have tested my invention,' he said moodily as he paced about the tiny room. 'That electronics firm wrote and told me they were willing to test my idea—and for a lot less than that con man fooled me into paying him. I've had nothing to do but work on it while I've been in Australia and I'm certain that it's a really viable commercial proposition. I'll just have to get another job and start saving up again, I suppose, but if I'd perfected a prototype I could have sold the patent to a big commercial company and we could have paid off Kiriakos,' he added wistfully.

'Kevin, do you really mean that?'

He raised his head, startled at the note of urgency in her voice. 'Why, yes. I've already approached a shipping company who've said they'll be interested to see it.'

Genista took a deep breath. 'Then—then I think I might be able to raise the money. No,' she raised a hand to stop his eager questions, 'don't ask me how. If I can raise it I'll get in touch with you and bring the money to you here.'

Kevin looked suspicious suddenly. 'You're not going to ask Kiriakos for it, are you? Because I'd rather. . . .'

'No.' Genista laughed bitterly. 'He's the last person I'd ever ask for anything.'

When she got home later that day, Genista unlocked the drawer of her dressing-table and took out the bracelet Marc had given her. She had worn it often, far preferring it to the more traditional style jewellery in the safe. It glittered back at her against the velvet as she ran a finger lingeringly over the leaves, realising just how fond she had become of it. She sighed, then shut the box with a snap; Marc had said it was hers and its monetary value could be the start of a new career for Kevin, one which he would enjoy and excel in for the rest of his life.

They had accepted an invitation to a cocktail party the next day and there was an official lunch the day after that, so it was some time before Genista could put her carefully thought out plan for disposing of the bracelet into operation. She arranged for the car to be at the door immediately after Marc had left for the office one morning and directed the chauffeur to take her to a large dress shop where she left him by the door. She tried on several things and bought two dresses which she had parcelled up for her. Casually she carried these across to the driver.

'Take these back to the car for me, please, Morent. And you needn't come back for another two hours. I'm going to wait here until a dress is altered to fit me.'

The man hesitated for a moment, then bowed slightly, only too glad to go about his own business instead of sitting in the shop reading the racing paper.

As soon as he had gone, Genista went back into a fitting room and changed into a pair of jeans and a shirt that she had brought with her crammed into a large handbag. Her other clothes she gave to a startled attendant. 'Would you put these into a bag, please, and when my chauffeur comes back tell him that he can have the rest of the day off. I shall be having lunch with my husband who will take me home.'

It was a big lie, and she just hoped that the chauffeur wouldn't check with Marc's secretary, but it was the only way she could think of that would give her several hours alone. She had no idea how long it would take to sell the bracelet and she was afraid her usual ploy wouldn't give her enough time.

Quickly she hurried through the streets, crowded with shoppers and tourists, making her way to the less fashionable quarter of Paris where there were many pawnshops who might take the bracelet. Genista knew that if she sold it she would probably get more money, but she had a strange reluctance to part with it completely and hoped to raise enough money by pawning it. No one took the slightest notice, other than a few appreciative male glances, at the slim, red-haired girl dressed in the casual denim uniform that typified all the young people in the streets. Her greatest fear had been how to avoid the pawnbroker learning her true identity, which was why she had changed her clothes; not even the most astute dealer would guess that a girl in faded denims was the wife of the wealthy Marc Kiriakos.

She shuddered at the thought of how the gossip columnists would seize on the story if she was recognised, and didn't even let herself think of what Marc's reaction would be. But then she pushed the thought from her mind; she would just have to make sure that no one did find out, that was all. Taking off her wedding ring, she put on a pair of large-lensed sunglasses before strolling as casually as she could into a likely-looking pawnshop. There were several people, mostly women, queueing up in front of her, chattering busily to each other as they waited. There was nothing furtive or shamefaced in their manner as there might have been in England, because the Parisian people of all classes made full use of the many pawnshops in the city, bringing their fur coats in to be stored for the summer, having the silver tea service put in the safe until the next time it was required, or pawning the family heirlooms to pay for a holiday.

When Genista's turn came she let it be understood that the bracelet had been given to her by a rich boy-friend, and tried to give the impression that hocking bracelets worth a small fortune was commonplace with her. The broker looked at it through a magnifying glass, read the name of the jeweller on the box, and had no hesitation in giving her a great pile of garishly coloured French notes in payment. Feeling almost sick with relief, Genista tucked the pawn ticket safely in her purse and then took a taxi to Kevin's flat. He immediately wanted to know where she had got the money and Genista smiled rather grimly at this reversal of their roles, but she fobbed him off and made him take all his drawings and papers and go there and then to the electronics firm.

After she had seen him off in the taxi she had used, Genista felt strangely flat, the adrenalin engendered by the last few hours slowing down and making her feel almost listless in comparison. She knew she ought to be getting back to the chateau, but it felt good to be alone and to wander down to the Seine and look at the artists' pictures set out on the left bank, to buy a savoury pancake from a *crêperie* and eat it with her fingers. A young, long-haired American tried to pick her up, talking to her in murdered French and looking astonished when she said, 'Thanks, but no, thanks,' in English. He accepted the rebuff goodnaturedly enough and suddenly Genista felt young again. She hadn't realised just how much of a strain her life with Marc had become; trying to live up to the standard he required of her and hold her place in society in this most demanding of cities, was hard enough, but when the part was a false one and opposite a man she actively disliked, the strain became almost intolerable.

A kind of recklessness filled her and she deliberately forgot about the chateau in her enjoyment of being alone. She spent ages in a drug store wandering round the counters and trying out all the perfume and make-up testers just like all the other girls. At about five in the afternoon she sat on a high stool at a counter and watched herself eating a hamburger and drinking a Coke in the mirrored wall opposite. She giggled to herself as she remembered the fashionable luncheon she had attended only the day before—if those important people could only see her now! But the thought made her remember that she had to go back to that world. Slowly she climbed down from the stool and went to find a taxi to take her back to it.

Paying off the taxi a few hundred yards away from the chateau, Genista made her way round the outside of the wall until she came to a small gate that the gardeners used as a short cut to and from the nearby village where they lived and which she knew wouldn't yet be locked for the night. Quickly she pushed it open and ran through the park to the edge of the trees where she paused to look at the house. There was no sign of life, so she ran breathlessly through the parterre and across the terrace into the drawing-room. Panting a little, she peeped into the hall. It, too, was deserted. She darted across in the direction of the staircase, but she had got only half way when she heard a door close behind her and then Marc's voice froze her in her tracks.

'Genista!' He came striding across and swung her round to face him. 'Are you all right? What happened to you?' Then his eyes took in her clothes and she felt her heart begin to pump with fear at the sudden look of fury that appeared on his face.

He dragged her into his study and slammed the door. Still holding her wrist, he pulled her across to his desk and picked up the phone. When his secretary answered he spoke curtly, telling him to have the search called off; Madame Kiriakos had returned to the chateau. Then he put down the receiver and turned to her, his eyes blazing with scarcely controlled rage. 'Where the hell have you been?' he asked savagely.

Genista stared back at him; there was no way in which she was going to tell him the truth, so the only thing to do was to brazen the thing out. Lifting her chin, she said contemptuously, 'Oh, really, all this fuss! If you must know I got sick to death of acting my part in this farcical half-marriage, so I took a day off. All your other employees are allowed some time off, so why not me?' She pulled her wrist from his suddenly slack grasp and went to move past him, but he barred her way.

'Did you go to meet someone?' he demanded, his anger, if anything, greater than before.

Her resentment added fire to her defiance. 'What if I did?' she taunted him. 'What's it got to do with you what the staff do on their days off?'

Almost before she had finished speaking Marc had caught hold of her by the shoulders, shaking her until she felt dizzy. '*Mon dieu*, I should like to....' His teeth clenched. 'You'll tell me the truth, *comprenez*?' His fingers bit into her shoulders and she winced with pain. 'Now. Who did you go to meet? Was it a man?'

Her defiance drained away. Genista looked slowly up at him. 'No. There was no one,' she said dully. 'I—I just wanted to be by myself, not to have the chauffeur following me everywhere I went.'

Marc looked at her searchingly until Genista turned her head away from his analytical regard. 'Is that the truth?' he asked, his voice harsh in her ears.

'Believe it or not, just as you like. I couldn't care less.' He let her go and she slumped into a chair, rubbing her shoulders.

Marc turned his back on her while he took two cigarettes from the silver box on his desk. He lit one and gave it to her, his hand briefly touching hers. Lowering his head, he lit his own and it was some seconds before he looked at her again. His rage had quietened now, but his lips were still a thin line in his set face. He drew on his cigarette, then said abruptly, 'Have you given Morent the slip before?'

Genista nodded reluctantly. 'Yes, but only for short periods.'

'He follows you on my orders. I'm sorry if you find it irritating, but it's for your own protection.'

She raised her eyebrows in surprise. 'Why on earth should I need protection?'

'To prevent your being kidnapped,' he replied in a clipped voice, adding at her look of amazement, 'Don't underrate the possibility, Genista. That particularly disgusting crime is unfortunately on the increase in France —I believe their latest pleasant little trick is to cut off the victim's little finger and send it through the post. You'd be worth millions in ransom to a kidnap gang.'

'But you don't care about me enough to pay a ransom,' she exclaimed impulsively.

His cigarette end glowed brightly. 'But they're not to know that, are they?'

'No, I suppose not.' She looked down at her hands. 'I'm sorry. I didn't mean to worry you. You should have explained to me before.'

He ground out his cigarette in the ashtray. 'Perhaps we've both been working too hard and need a holiday. How about if we went back to Akasia for a week or so?' Genista felt her whole body stiffen at mention of the island and she gripped the arms of her chair tightly. 'I thought perhaps we might ask Tante Mathilde to join us,' he added casually.

Her eyelids flew up and for a moment their glances

met before she hastily looked away again. 'That would be very—nice,' she said inadequately.

His aunt proved agreeable and within two days they were in Akasia where Genista gradually found the tensions beginning to ebb away as they lazed in the sun. A lot of the time she spent chatting with Madame de Frémond and they became on such good terms that Genista was invited to call her Tante Mathilde too. They sat together on the terrace, idly watching Marc and his Greek crewman prepare the *Aphrodite* for a trip to the island of Delos that they'd planned for the next day.

'Marc seems much more relaxed than I've seen him for a long time. I was beginning to despair of him ever falling in love again, so it made me very happy when he found you at last,' his aunt remarked, in obvious ignorance of the fact that she and Marc were using separate rooms.

'Again? Has he been—in love before, then?'

'Why, yes, did he not tell you?'

'No, but I always assumed that he couldn't have got to be thirty-five without having had some women in his past.'

'Oh, women, yes.' Tante Mathilde shrugged expressively. 'But only one love. He was very young at the time, of course. Still at university, and Adrienne at finishing school. Marc's father was against the marriage because Adrienne's family were among the lower aristocracy and very poor. He wanted more for his only son; a mistaken ambition, for it turned Marc against him when he refused his permission. Then Adrienne was married off to a rich, middle-aged marquis, which put the seal on Marc's bitterness. For a long time he was very unhappy, burying himself in his studies, and, after his father died, building up his business into the vast international empire it is today. I must admit that I always thought that if he couldn't have Adrienne he would have no one, so you can imagine my delight when he told me about you.'

Tante Mathilde smiled at her and Genista returned the smile woodenly, her mind racing. It explained so much in Marc that she had never understood before; the callousness he had shown in regard to her, the bitter look she had sometimes surprised on his face. Was he still hungering in his frustrated heart for the woman he had lost? It was true when his aunt said that he seemed relaxed enough now, but only Genista knew how much a front their marriage was for the real thing.

The sun was high in the sky overhead and Genista turned lazily on to her front to shut the glare from her eyes. She was lying on a thick towel spread on the cabin roof of the boat while it flicked its way carelessly through the gentle waves of the deep blue sea. Tante Mathilde had backed out of the trip at the last moment as she had a headache, but Genista could just see the top of the crewman's head as he stood at the wheel. Reaching out, she picked up a bottle of sun oil and began to rub it into her shoulders. She felt a movement nearby and then the bottle was taken from her hand as Marc squatted down beside her and started to rub the oil in himself.

'I brought you a drink,' he informed her.

She murmured her thanks and lay still, feeling his strong hands massaging the oil into her back. His touch was firm, yet oddly sensuous, making her fully aware of her own body. He undid the hook of her bikini top and let the straps fall to her sides. Instinctively she stiffened, but he said softly, 'Relax, you don't want to have a white mark when you put your evening dresses on, do you?'

His hands continued at their task, rubbing the oil into her legs right up to where the bottom half of her bikini started. 'Why don't you take the bottom half off and get an all-over tan?' he suggested. 'No one can see you.'

'Except you!' Genista replied tartly.

He spread himself out beside her and grinned. 'Except me, of course.'

'You're so expert at that oiling routine you must have had dozens of women sunning themselves up here,' she remarked caustically.

'Well, yes,' he admitted, 'But not more than two or three at a time!'

His grin broadened and suddenly Genista found that they were laughing together. Her face sobered first and she looked away, idly picking at the edges of the towel.

'It's good to get away for a while,' Marc murmured. 'Sometimes you can look at things more objectively from a distance.' He didn't enlarge on the remark but went on to tell her about Delos, the island they were on their way to visit, then passing on to other subjects, telling her anecdotes and making her laugh. He was less tense that she had ever known him and he put himself out to make her feel at ease too.

When they anchored in a bay of the island Genista changed into a sun-dress before they went ashore. It was a beautiful, ancient island, only six kilometres long by one wide and dominated by its sacred mountain, Kinthos. The doleful plucking of a mandolin followed them as they walked along the Sacred Way, flanked by the famous smiling stone lions that guard the three temples dedicated to Apollo, the sun-god, and his sister Artemis, the beautiful huntress who was the goddess of marriage and the bestower of fertility. Today there are no trees on Delos, but once it was full of trees and flowers and, as the most sacred island of ancient Greece, where no one was allowed to be born, to fall ill or to die, it had been embellished by sun-worshippers through the centuries with everything that money could buy. The Sacred Harbour and the Sanctuary and the Gymnasium were still there to see, but the sun-blanched open-air theatre, forty-three tiers high, was overgrown with weeds, and the mighty colossus of Apollo that had once towered majestically over the island was gone for ever.

The going was rough underfoot so that Genista almost tripped. Marc put his hand under her elbow to steady her and when she stumbled again it seemed only natural that he should take her hand to help her along. It was very hot and there was a sad, almost haunting air about the fallen sculptures, the mosaic floors and wall paintings that depicted a long-forgotten age. In its mystical quiet, disturbed only by the bleating of the goats, Delos was overwhelming, awe-inspiring.

They swam to cool themselves down and ate a picnic meal on the beach before setting out for Akasia again. Genista wandered into the cockpit and Marc dismissed the crewman and let her take the wheel for a while. It felt good to feel the throb of the powerful engines under her fingertips and she began to understand a little his love of sailing.

'There's a festival in Limani tonight,' Marc remarked. 'I thought we might go along there after dinner.'

The boat plunged slightly in the wash of another boat and she was thrown a little against him. The bare flesh of his chest felt hot against her arm. 'I'd like that. I've never been to a village festival before.' She tried to speak calmly, but she found that her breath was suddenly uneven.

For the visit to the festival she put on a modern version of the Greek national costume with a black off-the-shoulder blouse and a gaily coloured tiered skirt. Tante Mathilde resolutely declined their invitation to accompany them as she wished to listen to a concert on the radio; Genista wondered if this was just a tactful way to leave them alone together and didn't know whether to be pleased or sorry. The sun was setting as they walked along the path to the village, the sky tinged with the most improbable shades of red that brought a flush of life to the cold stone of the statue as they passed the temple.

Limani was much the same as every other village in the islands; white cubic houses, an arcaded chapel, roads flagged with whitewashed tiles, with here and there a brightly painted door or shutter. Marc led her to the taverna where he was greeted by cries of '*Cháirete*' and '*Kaliméra*', and people rushed to place chairs round a table for them. Marc saw her into her seat and then went round shaking hands with everyone. The men greeted him with affectionate respect while the women smiled shyly at him—all except one young girl who gazed boldly into his eyes, Genista noted wryly. Everyone seemed to be drinking ouzo or retsina and soon the music drew people on to the floor to dance the famous rhythmic *Sirtaki*, a basic dance form with an infinite variety of adaptations.

Marc came to sit beside her to watch and often introduced her to people who came up to their table. Soon she had lost count of the number of fishermen and their wives she had shaken hands with and the number of glasses of retsina she had drunk. It was mostly the men who were dancing now, their women sitting in groups, talking together. After a particularly intricate dance she went to applaud, but Marc stopped her, telling her that the Greeks regarded it as rude to do so. Some men began to call his name, asking him to get up and dance. At first he laughingly refused, but when they became insistent he got up and began to dance alone, slowly, his arms outstretched as he bent and swayed to the rhythm of the music. Gradually it began to get faster and the lower half of his body turned with it while his head and shoulders hardly moved at all. His feet stamped out the beat on the stone floor and then suddenly he threw his whole body into the dance, leaping, kicking his feet together in the air, his movements graceful and controlled and yet wild and primitive. Then the music stopped on a sudden high note, and he was being patted on the back and congratulated back to his seat.

It was shortly after this that he touched her arm and suggested it was time they left. There were shouts of 'Sas kalí níchta, goodnight,' as they threaded their way through the tables, and the bold-eyed girl deliberately placed herself in Marc's way so that he had to brush against her to get past. He glanced down at the girl with a touch of wry amusement in his face, but then they were through and outside in the clear night air. They strolled back in companionable silence, broken only by an odd remark now and then. When they got to the temple they stopped in mutual accord and turned to look across the beach to the sea, its gentle breakers effervescent in the moonlight.

'It's so peaceful,' Genista said dreamily. 'Just as if time

had stood still for a thousand years.' Looking up at the moon, she added on a rather wistful note, 'The only thing is, it makes you realise just how small and unimportant you are in the scheme of things. How insignificant all the things that worry you and make you unhappy really are.'

Marc turned towards her, his face thrown into relief by the moonlight. 'Are you so unhappy with me, Genista?'

She turned and walked a few steps apart from him. 'No, not really. I—I expect I've just had too much to drink and it's making me feel maudlin, that's all.' But even to her own ears her voice sounded brittle and unconvincing.

Coming to stand close beside her, Marc reached out and took hold of her arms, his grip gentle, his eyes trying to read hers in the darkness. When she moved to turn her head away, he said softly, 'No, don't shut me out. Tell me the truth. Are you so very unhappy?'

His hand lifted her chin so that she had to look at him, but Genista found that she couldn't speak and had to blink hard to prevent her eyes pricking with tears at his totally unexpected tenderness, a tenderness that he had never shown before and she had thought entirely alien to his nature. She tried to speak, but could only stare up into his eyes. He made a small sound in his throat, his hand moved to the back of her head and suddenly his lips were on hers, warm and firm as they explored her mouth. His arms came down to press her close against him and then he kissed her with a fierce, bruising intensity.

Genista was so taken aback that for a moment she stood passively within his arms, her brain whirling as her body became aware of the sensations his lips and his closeness were arousing in her. The realisation that these sensations were pleasant rather than repugnant shocked her and her automatic reaction was to become tense and rigid. Feeling her rigidity, Marc let go of her abruptly and took a pace backwards.

'I'm sorry,' he said shortly, his voice uneven. 'I shouldn't have done that. The night must have got to me too.' He ran a hand through his hair. 'I think I'd better have a swim to cool off. Are you coming?'

'No, I—haven't got a swimsuit.'

He laughed mirthlessly as he walked to a path leading down to the beach. 'So you haven't—but then who needs one?' He loped down the path and then turned back to look at her.

Genista stared down at him for a moment and then turned and began to hasten along the path to the villa, but at the first block of shadow thrown by the olive trees she stopped to look back. Marc's clothes were piled at the water's edge and he was wading naked into the sea, the moonlight bronzing his skin and giving him an unreal quality like the bronze statues of the ancient pagan gods. Slowly she walked back to the ruined temple and sank down on the grass at the base of the statue. Her mind felt numb and her mouth and body ached with the remembrance of his kiss. If she hadn't tensed up, if she had let him go on kissing her, would he have laid her here in the grass and made love to her at Aphrodite's feet?

She tried to convince herself that she was glad he had stopped, that his kisses were the last thing she wanted, but gradually her mind accepted the truth and she knew that if he had gone on kissing her for just a minute longer she would have responded. The realisation almost frightened her. How could one go from fierce hatred to —to this, in a few short months? Her hatred of him had been real enough, but lately, whenever she thought back to that night together on the island, it had been with very mixed feelings. She remembered the way he had described her own body to her, making love to her with his voice as well as his hands, and suddenly she was filled with a fierce yearning to have him touch her again. To touch her until he aroused in her a passion to match his own. She wanted him to love her until.... Love? Was that what she wanted? What she felt? The thought bewildered her for a moment, but she didn't attempt to analyse her feelings, just accepted them. The yearning, the need of him filled her. If she stayed here, if she waited for him, then perhaps...?

As Marc came out of the sea she felt herself begin to tremble with expectancy. He rubbed himself dry on his shirt, then dressed quickly. He began to climb up from the beach and Genista stood up in the shadow of the statue, her heart pounding, her throat so dry she couldn't speak. He stepped on to the track—then turned to the left and strode quickly away in the direction of the village.

For a moment Genista was too stunned to think, then a sharp, stabbing pain of jealousy filled her as she remembered the girl in the taverna who had smiled so boldly at him. Was he going to her? She gave a bitter little laugh. Why not? He just wanted a woman, and if he couldn't have the one at hand then the next one would do. She found that it hurt unbearably to think that he only wanted her physically. She tried to be sensible, to tell herself that he had never pretended anything else. Some woman once had found his elusive heart and pierced it, and now he treated all women with the same cruel arrogance, using them as he wanted them.

And she had been ready to give herself to him! The irony of it made her laugh aloud, but presently she sank to the ground again, her head against the statue's plinth. 'What shall I do, Aphrodite?' she murmured softly. 'How can I make him love me?' Her mood of despair slowly lifted. They were living under the same roof, were constantly in each other's company, weren't they? Perhaps proximity might gradually make him come to care for her. There might never be that ecstasy of an intensely emotional affair, but at least there could be happiness and contentment. But perhaps there was one other way; feeling rather silly, Genista got on her knees and dug a little hole with her fingers at the base of the statue. Taking a small brooch—one of her own trinkets—from her dress, she placed it in the hole and hastily covered it. 'Please make him love me,' she whispered, then got to her feet and ran back to the villa.

CHAPTER SEVEN

'*Pardonnez-moi, madame.*'

Genista looked up from the conversation she was having with the chef in the kitchen of the chateau as a maid sought her attention. 'Yes, Françoise? What is it?'

'Monsieur Kiriakos wishes to see you in his study.'

'Very well, I'll come at once.' She thanked the chef and walked unhurriedly away. She felt tired, but pleasantly so. Last night they had gone to a ball, their first since coming back to France, and this time she hadn't had to put on an act; her smiles had been real, the way she had moved into his arms when they danced, the look when he had kissed her hair, all had been meant. It had hurt a little that he was still only pretending, but perhaps he had sensed a change in her, a relaxing of tension, because he had seemed happier and more carefree. They had danced into the small hours, and he had held her close against him, her hand touching the silky hairs at the back of his neck, and they had been among the last to leave. Marc had said goodnight to her at her bedroom door, forgetting even to lock her jewels in the safe.

To her annoyance, Genista saw that Madame Hermant was in the study with Marc. She sighed; the housekeeper always went to Marc rather than to her. With a warm but rather shy smile for him, she said lightly, 'A domestic crisis?'

Marc smiled only briefly in return and his voice was cold as he said, 'Rather more than that. You asked

Madame Hermant to bring me the sapphires you were wearing last night to put in the safe?'

'Yes, I did.' Genista was filled with a sense of fore-boding as she looked at their faces. 'Why, what is it?'

'The earrings are missing, madame,' the housekeeper told her, her voice devoid of the satisfaction it would have shown if Marc hadn't been there.

'But—but they can't be! I know I had them when I got home. Marc, you must remember that I was wearing them in the car?'

He shook his head. 'You had your hair down and I didn't notice.'

'But they must be in my room. I'll go and look myself.' Genista turned to leave, but as she did so there was a knock on the door and the maid came in.

'We've found Madame's earrings,' the girl said, and Genista gave a little gasp of relief, glad that all the fuss had been for nothing. Crossing to Marc, the maid put them into his outstretched hand.

He bent to examine the jewels. 'Where did you find them?' he asked grimly.

'One was on the floor in the bathroom, Monsieur, but the other had gone partly down the waste pipe of the shower and I had to fetch Jacques to get it out. I'm afraid two of the stones came loose,' she added apologetically.

'Never mind, Françoise, you have done well. You may go,' he said, with one of his charming smiles for the maid.

Genista waited until she had gone out of the door and then turned swiftly to face him. 'Marc, I swear I took those earrings off before I showered. They couldn't poss....'

But he cut her short peremptorily, anger in his voice.

'You do yourself no good by these protestations. It was my fault as much as yours; I should have made sure that they were put in the safe immediately we arrived home. I will make certain we do so in future.'

'I beg your pardon, monsieur,' Madame Hermant put in, 'I am very glad that the earrings have been found, of course, but this has caused a great upset among the staff who were afraid they might be accused of having stolen them. So may I suggest, to avoid this happening again, that Madame also keeps her diamond bracelet in the safe?'

Genista felt suddenly very cold as she saw the neat trap that had been laid for her. The housekeeper must have noticed that she no longer wore the bracelet and could easily have seen that the case was no longer in her dressing-table—in fact Genista hadn't bothered to lock the drawer since she had pawned it.

'Yes, I think that's a good idea. You'd better fetch it to me, Genista.'

Her face white, Genista looked steadily at the housekeeper. 'Please leave us, madame.'

The woman gave a little nod and turned to go, a look of gloating spite on her face as she passed Genista.

There was no point in prevaricating, the truth had to be faced. 'I can't give you the bracelet, I haven't got it any more.'

Marc looked at her sharply, his eyes searching. 'What have you done with it?'

'I sold it,' she told him baldly.

He stared at her and a muscle in his jaw tightened. 'Would you mind telling me why?'

'I—I needed some money.'

'What for? What have you been up to?' With a swift

movement he came round the desk and stood menacingly in front of her. 'Tell me,' he ordered.

Genista backed away, frightened of his anger. 'I bought a lot of things and they came to more than I anticipated.' It was a poor effort but the best she could think of on the spur of the moment.

'*Mon dieu*, isn't the allowance I pay you enough? Have you so little regard for money that you allow yourself to get into debt?' he demanded angrily.

'You said that the bracelet was a gift to do as I liked with. You said it meant nothing to you!' Genista retorted.

'It means something to me when my wife gets into debt!' Marc returned caustically.

As angry now as he, Genista said impetuously, 'All right, I'll pay you for the damn bracelet.'

With a contemptous sneer, he asked, 'And just how do you intend to do that?'

'I'll work it off. You can extend the time I stay with you to cover it.'

'Be careful, Genista, at this rate you'll still be tied to me when you're ninety! But I'm afraid that isn't good enough, I want a more immediate repayment.'

Genista felt the flush of anger drain from her face. 'You know that I have nothing. Except....'

'Except?'

'Except myself,' she said slowly.

He stiffened. His eyes fastened on her face. 'Exactly what do you mean by that?' His voice sounded very odd.

'You—you know what I mean.'

'But let us be quite clear about this. You mean that you'll give yourself to me?'

'Yes.' She looked away from him, unable to bear his searching gaze.

'Willingly?'

'Y-yes.'

He paused. 'Then prove it,' he said softly.

Her eyes flew to his. 'What—what do you mean?'

'Show me just how willingly you'd come to me.'

'Now?' she asked jerkily.

'Why not now?'

Her eyes wide in the pallor of her face, Genista nerved herself to walk the few steps across the room to stand close in front of him. His eyes glinted down at her, his face expressionless as he stood still, waiting for her to make the first move. Slowly she raised her hands to rest them on his shoulders, then stood on tiptoe so that her face was level with his. When her mouth found his lips they were warm and sensuous against hers. She had expected him to take her in his arms and return her embrace with something of the intensity he had shown on the island, but as she continued to kiss him he made no move to touch her and his lips became cold and hard beneath her own. After a minute she lowered her arms and stepped back, looking down at the floor.

'What's the matter, Genista? Isn't it any fun kissing someone who turns to stone at your touch, who treats you like a leper?' His voice was hard, incisive, with an edge to it, and an unpleasant undertone of mockery.

Her face ashen, she went to turn away, but he said jeeringly, 'Was he going to pay you back this time, Genista?'

Swiftly she raised her eyes to look at him. 'How did you know?' she asked dully after a moment.

'It didn't take much working out. The news that your

brother had left his job in Australia and you needing a large sum of money—the two went together. What did he want it for this time, another miraculous invention?' She tried to answer, but he didn't give her time before going on exasperatedly, 'Genista, he isn't worth it. Can't you see that he's just a sponger? He'll live off you like a parasite and he won't give a damn about how you get the money so long as you get it. And you'd even sell yourself—for him!'

'That isn't true! Kevin didn't ask for the money. You just won't give him a chance,' she answered, defiant again in defence of her brother.

Marc continued to look at her angrily for a moment, but then his annoyance faded and he said, 'Why are you so loyal to him?'

Painfully she replied, 'I told you once before; Kevin is all I have.'

'You have me.'

'You?' Her eyes opened wide at that and she stared up at him, but she couldn't fathom the look in his eyes. 'No,' she said at last decisively. 'No, I don't.'

He straightened, his face a grim mask. 'Forget about the bracelet, but in future you'll come to me whenever you need money, do you understand?'

Reluctantly Genista nodded, while resolving never to do so. She turned to leave, but as her hand closed over the door knob his voice stopped her.

'And remember one thing, Genista. I don't buy my women. You belong to me and I could have taken you any time I'd wanted you—if I'd wanted you!'

For a long time Genista sat alone in her room, but at length she picked up the internal phone and told Madame Hermant that she wanted to see her. When the woman came Genista sat and looked at her before saying coldly, 'You have resented my presence in this house since the first day I came here. There can be no doubt that your position is assured, so there must be some other reason for the spiteful trick you played on me. And make no mistake, madame, I intend to find out what it is. You have made my life here extremely uncomfortable, but I in turn can make life unbearable for you if I have to,' she threatened.

The housekeeper sniffed disdainfully. 'Don't think you can frighten me with your high and mighty airs. You're not a lady and you will never learn to be one. Do you think I haven't noticed the way you've been behaving since you came back to France? You're falling in love with him, anyone can see that. But you're wasting your time,' she added sneeringly. 'Do you really think he would bother with you when he's been hopelessly in love with my mistress for years?'

'Your mistress?' Genista asked faintly.

'Yes, the Marquise d'Anyers. He fell in love with her years ago, but she was forced to marry the Marquis. Well, he's very ill now, and as soon as he dies she and Monsieur Kiriakos will marry,' she finished triumphantly.

'He can hardly have two wives!' Genista put in tartly.

The housekeeper laughed derisively. '*Pauvre imbécile!* Do you think he cares about you? The gossips had started to link their names, but Monsieur wouldn't have a hint of scandal attached to my mistress's name, so he married you to kill the gossip, a nobody that he could get rid of as soon as the Marquis dies!'

Genista rose slowly to her feet and went to the window, turning her back on Madame Hermant. 'Why do you call her your mistress?' she asked at length.

'Because I've worked for her family ever since she was a child. She's so lovely, so beautiful, and to have her beauty wasted on that decrepit old man—it's a cruel shame. When Monsieur Kiriakos inherited this chateau and needed a housekeeper, she asked me to come and I was glad to do it for her sake, knowing how much she loved him.'

'I see.' Genista turned to face her. 'You've made your position very clear. You may go about your duties that you carry out so—efficiently.'

The woman looked at her suspiciously. 'If you take my advice you'll go away and. . . .'

'I don't need your advice, madame, and so long as I am still the chatelaine in this house you will obey my orders. I've said you may go.'

With another disapproving sniff, the housekeeper walked briskly from the room, slamming the door shut behind her. Dizzily Genista continued to stare at the door, unable to take in all that she had heard. She felt almost sick with humiliation, first from Marc's rejection of her and now this. The knowledge that he was just using her until the woman he loved was free was the bitterest thing that had ever happened to her. She sat down at her desk and put her head in her hands. She had hoped for so much, had glimpsed a possible future of happiness with Marc, and now, to be told—quite definitely—that he cared nothing for her made her heart ache with unhappiness. But she wouldn't cry, she wouldn't! She bit her knuckles hard, the physical pain somehow blunting the other pain and stopping the tears that threatened to flow down her cheeks. She ought to be glad; glad that she had always resisted him and that he had rejected her earlier. The thought that she might have given herself to him when he cared nothing for her filled her with bitter self-contempt. More than anything she longed to get away from him, to end this farcical charade that they were playing. But she was trapped; trapped by her own sense of honour that wouldn't let her walk out on him until she had repaid her debt, even though she now knew that he had married her for the most contemptible of reasons. Everything would just have to go on as it had before, only this time when she smiled and laughed at parties the pretence would be harder than ever, with the added misery of knowing that the part Marc played was an even falser act than she had thought him capable of playing.

People did survive emotional catastrophes, even if they hardened in the process, and somehow she was going to survive, even if she became as hard and ruthless as he!

If Marc noticed any difference in her manner he must have put it down to their recent quarrel, but he didn't mention it. He was invariably polite to her in private, and in public continued to behave like a man who was, if anything, even more enraptured with her, so that sometimes she found it hard not to laugh in his face when he made some especially loving gesture; the irony of the situation would have been funny if it hadn't been so cruel.

The one small oasis of cheer in her desert of despondency was a call from Lyn to say that she was again in Paris. As before, they met at the airport restaurant, and Genista was surprised and pleased to see that her friend had a glow of radiance about her as she hurried up to greet her.

'Hey, you look like a million dollars!' Genista exclaimed. 'Have you scooped the jackpot on Ernie or just been chosen as the stewardess of the year?'

'Neither,' Lyn laughed happily. 'Look!' And she held up her left hand so that Genista could see the diamond solitaire that glittered on her third finger.

'Lyn! You don't mean that you and Paul are engaged? Why, that's wonderful!' Genista hugged her enthusiastically. 'I couldn't be more pleased. Come and tell me all about it.'

They found a table and soon Lyn was telling her the full story. Genista tried to keep her face pleased and interested, but she wouldn't have been human if she hadn't compared Lyn's bright future with her own bleak and unsettled one.

'So the wedding is to be next spring and you're invited, of course,' Lyn finished, then paused before reaching out to put a hand over Genista's. 'What is it, Gen? You're not jealous about Paul and me, are you? You don't still...?'

'Good heavens, no,' Genista hastened to reassure her. 'I'm sorry, did it show? No, I was just wishing that....' For a moment she toyed with telling Lyn of Marc's real reason for marrying her, but she pushed the idea aside; it was her own private hell. 'It's nothing. Go on, tell me what your parents think. Do they like Paul?'

But Lyn refused to be put off. 'Don't tell me there's nothing wrong when I can see that you're feeling wretched. Gen, if you're so unhappy why don't you leave him? You can always come back to the flat, you know that.'

'Thanks.' Genista's voice was unsteady and she struggled to control it. 'But I can't leave him, not while I still owe him money. So let's just forget about my troubles, shall we?' she went on determinedly. 'Where are you planning to go for your honeymoon?'

Reluctantly Lyn let herself be drawn back into their previous topic, but there were some misgivings in her face when they finally said goodbye an hour or so later.

'Gen, you're sure you're all right? Look, I know I'm putting this badly, but if you ever need any help—to get away from him, or anything—well, you know I'm on your side, and Paul will help too.'

'Yes, I know. Thanks, Lyn. Just keeping in touch helps a lot—more than you know.' She gave Lyn a quick hug, then turned to hurry back to the hairdressing salon, afraid that she might have been missed, but Morent was still sitting in his customary chair, reading the paper.

Slowly Genista began to come to terms with the situation; her own feelings she managed to keep under control and conceal beneath a veneer of cool reserve, and gradually, because he still discussed some aspects of his business with her, she began to relax again in Marc's company and take a renewed interest in their entertaining. Aly arrived back in Paris and this helped a lot, for it often meant that they went out as a foursome, the other girl being any one in a number of Aly's current girlfriends.

But Genista's fragile hold on something approaching normality was abruptly shattered one day in September when they had gone with a party of people to the races as Aly's guests. There had been a luxurious picnic lunch washed down with magnums of champagne and afterwards Aly had taken her to place bets on the races, insisting on giving her the money to do so. As they were returning to the box, Genista noticed that Marc was talking to a stranger, a fashionably dressed and very beautiful blonde woman of about thirty, who was lightly holding his arm and laughing up at him as he leaned down to talk to her.

Perhaps it was some sixth sense, perhaps only a tightening of Aly's hand under her elbow, but she felt no great surprise when Marc caught sight of her, hesitated for a moment, then said slowly, 'Genista, this is an old friend of mind, Adrienne, Marquise d'Anyers. Adrienne, this is my wife.'

The woman turned to give her a lazy smile, her glance flicking over her, taking in every detail. 'How nice to meet you at last. Genista. Marc has told me so much about you ... and I see that he described you very accurately.'

There was a note of amusement in her soft voice and despite herself Genista flushed as she realised just what that description must have been.

'Have you placed your bets? Which horses have you chosen?' Marc deliberately came to stand beside her, drawing her to the front of the box where they could lean out and watch the crowds of racegoers below them. For a bewildering moment it seemed as if he was glad to get away from the Marquise, but then Genista remembered bitterly that the whole purpose of marrying her was to prevent any scandal being attached to the Marquise's name. She stared fixedly across the racecourse and only answered him in monosyllables.

'What is it, Genista? What's wrong?' Marc's hand came down to covers hers on the rail, but she quickly snatched it away.

Pulling herself together, she assumed her bright, artificial smile and was able to ignore the speculative frown on his face as she said gaily, 'Why, nothing. Tell me, have you never been interested in owning racehorses?' She chattered on as if she hadn't a care in the world and gradually his frown lessened, but she was profoundly glad when someone came up to interrupt them and she saw that the Marquise had left the box to rejoin her own party.

A casual question to a fellow guest elicited the information that the Marquise had just arrived in Paris, unaccompanied by her husband who had remained behind at their chateau in Provence. Genista caught sight of her several times during that long afternoon and was able to see with startling clarity just why Marc had stayed so faithful to her through the years. For the Marquise was very lovely; small and slight, she had a delicate bone structure that gave her an air of fragility which must have roused the protective instincts in any man she met, and made Genista feel tall and gauche in comparison. Already there were several men hovering around her and Genista could only imagine Marc's feelings as she more than once caught him looking grimly in the Marquise's direction. Genista wondered with a sick feeling if Adrienne d'Anyers had come to Paris because Madame Hermant had told her that she was falling for Marc. Had she come to make sure that Marc still loved her, that Genista wouldn't be a threat to their plans? But the older woman's contemptuous smile when they had met had instantly dismissed Genista as being of little danger, so now she had only to re-arouse Marc's longing for her, to make sure that he stayed faithful for the short time that her husband was rumoured to have left to live. And then? Then Marc would kick Genista out, her usefulness over. He would do it politely, of course, probably making it seem as if he were doing her a favour. Perhaps he might even pay her alimony—a sort of redundancy payment, she thought with bitter irony.

The Marquise was much in evidence at most of the functions they attended over the next two weeks, but Marc was so careful to keep out of her way, to pass no more than a greeting when they did meet, that Genista almost began to hope that Madame Hermant had been wrong after all and that Marc was no longer interested. If anything, he seemed to be paying more attention to herself, in private as well as in public, involving her more in his work by taking her to see the yards where his ships were built.

'I've decided to enter the cruise ship business,' Marc told her as he pointed to a great steel hulk that already showed its graceful, sweeping lines. 'This is to be the first of three ships. When she's finished perhaps you'll launch her for me?'

Genista turned to face him; the shipyard was noisy with thudding hammers and the loud clang of rivet guns, but she was deaf to everything except his words. 'When do you think she'll be ready?' she asked slowly.

'In about six months, I should think. Early next spring.'

Six months. Yes, it might take that long for the Marquis to die. She turned to look back at the boat. 'What do you intend to call her?' she asked dully.

He came to lean his hand against a piece of scaffolding. 'I thought I'd name her after you. The *Madame Kiriakos*,' he said quietly.

Her head came round sharply at that and she stared into his dark eyes. 'But—that's only a temporary title,' she managed at last.

Marc straightened up and moved towards her, his eyes intense. He went to say something, but she only caught, 'It's as per....' when there was a terrific noise that cut across his words as the high, screeching whine of an oxy-acetylene cutter started up nearby. They escaped to the comparative quiet of the shipyard offices, but there were people there who claimed his attention, and when they were alone again he was busy sorting out various problems that had arisen, dictating into an audio unit as they were driven along.

Unbelievably, it seemed to Genista, the Marquise's coming to Paris seemed only to make Marc spend more time at home. She had expected him to slip away so that he could meet the woman he loved in secret, but he mostly worked in his study at the chateau, and if he had to go elsewhere often took her with him. He seemed to seek her company and if she hadn't known that he was crazy about the Marquise she could almost have believed that he had begun to care for her.

'I've got a problem, Genista, and I need your help,' he remarked one morning as they were breakfasting on the terrace. It was probably one of the last days they would be able to do so, for already the leaves on the trees were beginning to change to yellow and orange and the sun had lost the intense heat of high summer.

Genista raised her eyebrows. 'You have a problem you can't solve yourself?' she asked in surprise.

'Oh, I always bow to the experts,' he told her. 'And in this case you're the most expert person I know.' He caught the sceptical glance she gave him. 'C'est vrai,' he grinned, then more seriously, 'I'm backing a new scientific technique and it's important that the right people are told about it, preferably all at the same time. I've had a film made that explains the technique, but rather than send each individual a copy, I want to invite them to a collective showing in Paris. But it occurs to me that they might be bored at the thought of spending time sitting in a cinema, and their wives most certainly would. So what do you suggest? How can I make them interested enough to see the film and keep their wives happy at the same time?'

'What you need is a captive audience,' Genista remarked. Then, an idea occurring to her, she asked, 'How important is this to you? And how many people do you want to invite?'

'About a hundred people, I should think. And it's very important. It could open up a whole new field of industry if I can convince enough people to give it sufficient backing.'

Genista leaned forward across the table. 'Then why don't you hire a plane? They have all the equipment for showing films, and afterwards you could throw a mid-air party. That way the guests would have something unusual to look forward to and you would have the captive audience you want for your film.'

'Yes, I see what you mean. It's a very good idea, Genista, and I'll get my secretary working on it right away. What sort of plane do you suggest?'

They continued to talk it over for some time until Marc rose to go to his study. Glancing at his watch, he remarked, 'I've just time to get this set up before I get ready for the charity polo match this afternoon.' His glance ran over her. 'You are coming along, aren't you?'

'To cheer you on?' she asked lightly.

He smiled slightly, his expression quizzical. 'I shall probably need it, I haven't played for months.' He reached down and casually took her hand in his, lightly running his finger over it. 'Won't you come along and give me moral support?'

'Yes, all right, if you want me to.'

'I do want you.' His grip tightened and for a heart-stopping minute she found herself looking directly into his eyes.

Abruptly she took her hand away and stood up. 'I'd better change, then.' She turned and hurried into the house leaving Marc looking pensively after her.

Shouts of encouragement went up from the spectators as Marc's team came galloping down the field, their polo mallets making loud cracking noises as they clashed with the opposing side. Aly had kindly explained the rules to her, but Genista found that she wasn't concentrating on the game; she was content to just sit and watch Marc as he sat astride a black pony, handling it well despite his professed lack of practice. Her thoughts were full of him and she didn't even try to put them out of her mind. This morning, when he had taken her hand, she could so easily have turned to him instead of away from him, so easily let him see that she wanted him. And she did want him, so much that it was like having a smouldering fire inside her, a fire that could be brought to flame by one kiss, one caress. And then goodbye to all the stubborn pride that held her back, her refusal to give herself to a man who didn't love her, loved some-one else. But did he? Again and again she asked herself the question. He had never shown any preference for the Marquise's company; she was here today and he had given her only a brief bow in passing. After all, she had only Madame Hermant's word to go on, and the housekeeper had shown how much she resented her. Could she have exaggerated, or even made up the story completely so that Genista would be unhappy, go away?

There was another great roar from the crowd, but Genista hardly took any notice. She sat back, her eyes troubled, as she tried to think the thing through. Beside her, Aly suddenly jumped to his feet with a shout of alarm. Startled, she turned her head to look and then froze with horror. The black pony was lying on the ground, struggling to get up, and Marc's still form was lying underneath it. Other riders dismounted and ran across to pull the horse to its feet. They bent over Marc and then one of them signalled for a stretcher to be brought and they lifted his unconscious body on to it.

Without knowing how she got there, Genista found that she had pushed her way down the stand and was running out of the exit, Aly pounding after her. She looked wildly around. 'Which way? Where will they take him?' she shouted frenziedly.

'To the first-aid room in the pavilion. It's right round the other side of the field. Come on!'

He took her arm and they started to run round the outside of the stands as behind them they heard the shouts of the crowd as the game recommenced. They were both panting for breath ten minutes later when they got to the pavilion, but Genista ran uncaring up the steps and pushed open the door. A uniformed first-aid man was coming down the corridor and she ran up to him. '*Monsieur—mon mari*, Monsieur Kiriakos, *ou est-il?*'

The man looked slightly surprised, but pointed to a door farther down the corridor. She hurried to it, but found that she was trembling so much that she couldn't turn the handle and Aly had to reach past her and push the door open. Stepping into the room she saw that Marc was lying on an examination couch, his head bandaged. But he wasn't alone. Leaning over him, her hair masking his face, was Adrienne d'Anyers. She was kissing him passionately, and even as Genista watched, Marc's arms came up and he put them round her.

Blindly she turned away, almost pushing Aly aside. He stared in amazement at her white face, took a quick look into the room, and then closed the door softly, his expression grim. She didn't remember Aly walking her out of the pavilion and to the bar, but after he'd made her drink a large brandy she gradually came back to life, outwardly at least, for there was a numbness deep inside her that was as yet too raw to even think about. Looking up from her drink, she found Aly's eyes, full of concern, on her face. He looked so worried that she stretched out her hand to him. His fingers closed tightly, painfully, over hers.

'Aly, will you do something for me?'

'Of course, anything,' he answered instantly.

'Will you lend me your car? And will you tell Marc that I had a migraine and left the match some time before his accident?'

He started to protest, but then fell silent and gave her his car keys. 'All right, *chérie*.' He shook his head sadly. 'What a mess! You should never have found out that way.'

'You—you knew?' Genista asked jerkily.

'I knew they had been lovers once, yes, but I thought it was all over years ago. I'm sorry, *ma petite*.'

'Don't be. There's nothing to be sorry for. But Aly, please don't say anything to Marc. I'd rather he didn't know.'

Reluctantly he gave his word before escorting her to his car. 'You're sure you're all right to drive?' he asked anxiously. 'You're not going to do anything crazy?'

'No,' she assured him. 'The only crazy thing I did was to fall in love with my own husband!'

On arriving at the chateau, Genista went straight to her room, giving orders that she wasn't to be disturbed and locking the door behind her. She undressed and lay in bed, gazing at the ceiling. She heard a car arrive and the sound of voices in the hall, then the throaty roar of the Ferrari as Aly drove away. Later footsteps sounded outside her room and there was a soft tap at the door. 'Genista,' Marc called her name but she didn't answer, turning her face into the pillow lest she start to cry and he heard her sobs, and presently she heard him go away.

The next two weeks she remembered only as days of increasing unhappiness. The knowledge that Marc was using her and that she had to stay with him until he had no further need of her was like a continuously spreading wound that refused to heal. Somehow she had managed to greet him the next day and make suitable exclamations about his accident. He had already removed the bandage and had a plaster dressing on his forehead, almost covered by a lock of dark hair. He showed concern for her headache and believed her when she pretended that she still wasn't feeling well and went back to her room almost immediately.

But she couldn't go on pretending because the next day Marc wanted to call a doctor and it was only by saying that she was feeling slightly better that she was able to dissuade him. So they again began to attend social functions together, but now Genista found that she couldn't act any more, couldn't keep the unhappiness out of her eyes. Twice they encountered Adrienne d'Anyers, but Marc's attitude towards her was more brusque than ever. That he could be like it amazed Genista, until she realised that if he was capable of playing one part to protect the Marquise's name from scandal, then he was also capable of playing the much harder one of pretending not to love her.

Feeling herself enmeshed in his sordid lies and duplicity, Genista let herself drift into a state of miserable apathy. There was nothing she could do, she could only go on as she was until the slender thread of the Marquis's life was broken and they had no further use for her. She didn't feel like eating and couldn't sleep. At one party she drank far too much, but it didn't even make her tipsy, only made her feel lonely and bitter. Almost desperately she took yet another glass from a passing waiter and lifted it to her mouth to drink down in one swallow.

Marc's hand closed over her wrist like a vice and forced her arm down. 'I think you've had enough,' he said grimly as he took the glass from her.

Taking a hanky from her bag, Genista dabbed at the few drops of liquid that had spilled on her dress. 'I'm not drunk,' she replied coldly.

'No, but you're trying to be. I think I'd better take you home,' he added shortly when she didn't answer.

'I can go alone. I'll send the car back for you. After all, you don't want to miss the chance of making a useful contact, do you?' she added with bitter sarcasm.

His jaw tightened and his eyes stared down at her angrily, but he didn't say anything, just took her arm and led her to their hostess, where he apologised charmingly for their premature departure. But once back at the chateau he led her inexorably into the drawing-room even though she tried to pull away.

'I have a headache. I want to go to my room.'

'Oh, no, not until you've told me just why you're behaving like this,' he said, his voice angry.

'I told you, I have a headache. I thought it might go away if I had a few drinks.'

He put his hands on her shoulders and looked down at her appraisingly. She was wearing a black evening dress that left her shoulders bare and the warmth of his hands on her skin made her quiver so much that he felt it. He said more gently, 'Something's happened to upset you, make you unhappy. Won't you tell me what it is?'

Biting her lip, Genista turned her head away and shook it miserably. 'It's nothing. Please let me go.'

Marc swore softly and said in angry exasperation, 'Why won't you confide in me? Haven't you yet learnt that you can trust me?'

'Trust you?' Genista stared at him, his words almost depriving her of speech. Then she said venomously, 'You're the last person I'd ever trust!'

'*Mon dieu*, are you never going to forget that night? What do I have to do to convince you that I...?'

'Forget it?' she broke in furiously. 'My God, how could I ever forget that, or the way you've used me since?'

'Then here's something else that you won't forget in a hurry!' Marc said savagely as he pulled her to him, his lips finding hers in a hungry, bruising passion that forced her head back until she could hardly breathe. For a moment the room whirled round her and then her body seemed to burst into flame as she responded to his kiss, arching her body against his, her hands locked in his hair as she pulled him yet closer to her.

'Genista!' Her name was no more than an amazed whisper in his throat as his lips explored the curve of her cheek, her eyelids, her throat, before returning to ravage her lips.

She moaned softly, some deep longing inside her making her body move sensuously against his as he held her close against him. He gave a kind of groan, his breathing ragged and uneven. He pulled down the strap of her dress and his hand sought her breast, followed closely by his lips. 'Oh, *ma belle*,' he began hoarsely. '*Si tu connaitrais combien....*'

The sound of his voice penetrated to her mind and it was as if she suddenly awakened from a wonderful dream. She stepped away from him, a look of horror in her eyes. 'What—what are you doing? Leave me alone. Oh, God, I must have been mad!' With trembling fingers she straightened her clothing, her eyes wide and frightened.

'Genista, don't be afraid, my little love.' He stepped forward to take her in his arms again.

The endearment, knowing as she did how false it was, revolted her. Drawing back from him repugnantly, she said fiercely, 'Don't touch me! I can't bear it when you handle me. You're—you're repulsive!' And then she turned and ran out of the room leaving him looking after her, his face grim, remote, frightening.

CHAPTER EIGHT

THE shrill sound of the telephone woke her the next morning. Sunlight filtered through the curtains and when she looked at her watch she saw that it was already eleven o'clock. It was Marc's secretary on the line, confirming the last-minute arrangements for their flying film show, which was due to take place the next day. Her head was thudding, but she managed to concentrate and answer his queries. Afterwards she showered under the cold tap to try to wake herself up. As she towelled herself dry she glanced in the mirror and stopped abruptly; the bruises from Marc's handling of her still showed on her breast, bringing her back with a sickening thud to reality.

Hardly had she finished dressing before the phone rang again and the butler informed her that a Monsieur Grey had called to see her and was waiting in the morning-room. Quickly she slipped on some shoes and ran down to meet him.

Kevin was striding up and down the room, a look of distaste on his face as he gazed up at the portraits on the walls. 'How on earth can you live in this place?' he greeted her. 'It's like a mausoleum!'

'Well, it's better than being surrounded by test-tubes and Bunsen burners all the time,' she retorted as he reluctantly allowed her to kiss him on the cheek.

'But I won't have to now, because I'm going to have my own laboratory,' he told her exultantly, his whole manner bursting with excitement.

'Kevin! You haven't—you haven't sold the invention?' she breathed.

'Haven't I just! They went potty over it and gave me a lump sum and a percentage of future sales, and what's more they've offered me a job in their research laboratories,' he finished triumphantly.

'Oh, Kevin, that's fantastic. You genius!' She threw her arms round him and hugged him so tight that he went red in the face.

'Hey, steady on! Don't you want to hear how the trials went? We took the device to....'

'Never mind that,' Genista broke in. 'How much did you get?'

He grinned. 'More than enough to cover the money that chap swindled me out of, and the money you gave me for the prototype. Look, I've brought my cheque book. We can write out a cheque for the money and leave it for Kiriakos. Go and pack your things while I write it out and leave him a note. I've got a car outside and we can leave right away. You won't ever have to see him again.'

Genista stared at him incredulously. 'Oh, Kevin!' And suddenly, stupidly, she found that she was crying.

'Don't cry, Gen. Please don't cry.' Awkwardly he tried to comfort her, rather aimlessly patting her back.

Sniffing hard, she smiled through her tears. 'I'm all right, really. It's just such a—a relief to know that I'm free.' Sitting down in a chair, she tried to think coherently. 'But it's not so easy to leave as that. He's got my passport locked in his safe, for one thing.'

'Well, ask him for it,' her brother said impatiently.

She shook her head. 'He wouldn't give it to me. You see, I'm still useful to him at the moment and he won't want to let me go just yet.' Frowning, she tried to think of some way round the problem, then her brow cleared as she remembered the mid-air party. Quickly she explained. 'He'll have to give me my passport then because I'm not a French citizen and will have to go through a different Customs gate.'

'And I'll be waiting with the car to take you to my flat,' Kevin added excitedly.

'No, I'd have to get right away. If I stayed in France Marc would be sure to find me,' Genista said with certainty. 'But I have other friends I used to work with who'll probably be able to help me to get out of the country.' She thought for a moment and then said, 'Look, Kevin, I pawned a bracelet to get the money for your prototype. If I give you the ticket will you go back to Paris and redeem it and then come back here? Oh, and get cash for the money you owe; he might tear up a cheque. In the meantime I'll pack a couple of suitcases with my own things. When you come back don't go through the main gate, there's a small door in the wall at the side of the chateau; I'll smuggle my cases out and meet you there.'

She explained more fully and then got the pawn ticket from her room. 'Here it is. I'll meet you at four o'clock. You can be back by then, can't you?'

Kevin assured her that he could and went off, the boyishness in him enjoying the clandestine nature of her escape. Genista watched him go and then picked up the phone and dialled Lyn's number. Madame Hermant, she knew, had gone shopping, so there was no danger of being overheard. When the call was answered she said urgently, 'Lyn, it's Gen. I've decided to leave him and I need your help. . . .'

The big Boeing that Marc had chartered for the evening came crisply in to land back in Paris just after midnight. The guests were laughing and it was quite noisy in the plane as they prepared to leave. The film show had been successful and the champagne party afterwards even more so. That, and the high altitude, seemed to have gone to the heads of quite a few people and there was some good-natured confusion as they made for the exits. Genista hung back to let the others pass, her heart beating fast as the moment of escape approached. She felt a touch at her elbow and turned to see Aly smiling down at her. It had also been a sort of farewell party for him because his own executive jet plane was waiting for him on the tarmac to whisk him back to Africa.

'Aren't you coming with the others to see me off?' he asked her.

She shook her head. 'No, I don't like public goodbyes.'

'Not goodbye, just au revoir. I'll be back in France in a couple of months,' he reminded her.

But Genista knew, sadly, that she would never see him again. Putting her hands on his shoulders, she reached up and kissed him gently. 'Goodbye, Aly,' she murmured.

Something in her voice must have alerted him because he put his arms round her and said quickly, 'Genny, what is it? What are you going to do?'

She shook her head, her eyes misty, then something made her glance across the plane. Marc was standing by the exit, ostensibly ushering out their guests, but now his eyes, cold as steel, were fastened on them as she still stood in Aly's arms. Quickly she disengaged herself, and when she looked again Marc had left the plane.

Genista was the last to leave, and as she passed the stewardess she gave her a small package. 'Monsieur Kiriakos forgot to take this with him. Will you see that he gets it after Sheik Fahid has left, please?' Then she was down the steps and on the tarmac, her bag containing her passport clutched in her hand. The others were moving in chattering groups through the alternate pools of darkness and light thrown by the overhead lamps, towards Aly's plane. Looking quickly round, she saw a caterer's van drawn up a few yards away in the giant shadow cast by the Boeing. A hasty look to make sure that she wasn't observed, and then she ran towards the open doors of the van.

'Gen?' Lyn leaned forward and pulled her inside while someone ran round to close the doors behind her. Then they were speeding across the airport while Genista hastily changed out of her dress and put on her old Globe Airways uniform.

'There isn't much room, I'm afraid, but it's the best we could do. Have you got your passport?' Lyn asked anxiously.

'Yes, it's in my bag.'

'What are you going to do with the dress?'

'I don't know. Get rid of it somewhere, I suppose.'

'Gen, it's a Dior! You can't just throw it away. Oh, here, give it to me, I'll roll it up and put it in your flight bag. Here's your shoes.'

Deliberately Lyn kept her talking, didn't give her time to think, to be afraid, and soon they had come to a stop beneath the wing of another jet, but in the familiar insignia of Globe Airways this time. The driver let them out, a sum of money changed hands, and then they were on board, both strapping themselves into the stewardesses' seats. There were a few harrowing moments of waiting before they were given clearance, but then the plane was taxiing to the runway, there was a jerk as the main wheels left the ground and then they were airborne at last.

Slowly Genista relaxed and glanced out of the window at the lights of Paris fast disappearing below them. She could hardly believe that it was all over; that she was free and need never see Marc, never watch him basely pretend that he cared for her, again. She wondered what his reaction would be when he opened the package and found the bracelet he had given her, the money that Kevin had borrowed, and a bank statement showing that she hadn't touched a franc of the allowance he had paid in for her. Apart from the clothes she had been wearing, she had taken nothing that he had given her. Her glance fell on her left hand. Except her wedding ring; that still shone bright and new on her finger. Raising her other hand, she went to remove it, then slowly drew back. No, she would wear his ring for a little longer, until the tie with Marc was completely broken.

Autumn passed into early winter, but Genista hardly noticed it as she resumed her old job and passed from climate to climate. It was nearly two months since she had left Marc and he had made no attempt to contact her through the airline. Several times she had seen his name mentioned in the papers in a business connection, and soon after she left there had been a picture of him arriving in Africa for a meeting, his face unsmiling, almost gaunt. After that she got in the habit of scanning the papers for any news of him and one day her eyes caught a familiar name in the obituaries column. It announced the death of the Marquis d'Anyers who had died at his home in Provence, deeply mourned by his widow, Adriénne.

That night she wrote to Marc's solicitors in Paris advising them that she would comply with any arrangements Marc wanted to make for a divorce so that he could be free to marry the Marquise. Her address she gave as care of Globe Airways headquarters in London. She had put her name down for as many flights as she could, hoping to make work the panacea to cure the numb ache in her heart, an ache that must surely, eventually fade away. Every time she flew back to London she expected to find a letter from his solicitors waiting for her, but for nearly two weeks now there had been nothing.

Perhaps there will be something this time, she thought as she stacked trays in the galley on a flight from Athens to New York. She had been serving the economy class, having lost seniority because she had left the company. Her fellow stewardess, a dark-haired, rather flippant girl, joined her.

'Well, that's the duty-free finished. Now perhaps we can have some peace for an hour or so before we serve dinner. What are the economy class like? I've already had two passes made at me,' she added with some satisfaction before Genista could answer. 'One wasn't bad, but the other—yeuk! But then that's how airline hostesses are, as everybody knows; always ready to hop into bed! But there's one guy in my section—now if *he* asked me. . . .' She went chattering on, Genista only half listening, until the girl happened to look out of the galley and said, her voice excited, 'Hey! That dishy guy I told you about—he's coming down here.' Her voice changed again, becoming low and husky as she said, 'Can I help you, sir?'

'Thank you, no.'

Only three words, but they made Genista drop the tray she was holding and turn to stare at Marc standing tall in the doorway.

'Hallo, Genista,' he said quietly.

The other girl looked at them as they stood with their glances locked, then she said quickly, 'I think I'll go up to the crew's quarters for a while,' and left them alone.

Her going brought Genista back to reality. She bent to retrieve the tray and stood with her back to him. 'What a coincidence. Are you going to New York on business?'

Marc stepped inside the galley and pulled the curtain closed behind him. 'It's no coincidence. I took this flight because I knew you'd be on it.' His voice sounded tight, unnatural.

'You needn't have bothered to see me yourself. Your solicitors could have handled the divorce.' She reached for another stack of trays, but his hand closed over her wrist, making her still. 'Why have you come to see me? What do you want?' she asked after a moment, her eyes on his hand where it held her wrist prisoner.

'I want to know why you thought I would want to marry Adrienne d'Anyers,' he said grimly.

'Oh, is that all? Because I was told so. Quite definitely. Madame Hermant told me a long time ago. She was afraid I might get ideas about wanting to be your wife permanently, so she let me know that you were just using me as a makeshift until the Marquise was free to marry you,' Genista told him, bitterness creeping into her voice although she tried to bite it back.

'And you ran away because you thought I was in love with her?'

'No, because I don't like being used!' she retorted shortly, and pulled her wrist away.

'I have no intention of marrying Adrienne, Genista. I admit I loved her once, but it was merely infatuation, a boyish calf-love that didn't last. I was already beginning to see her for what she was when she married the Marquis for his money and title. I had nothing much to offer her then, you see, only expectations, but she was impatient, so she jilted me for a better catch. Any feelings I might still have had for her died very soon after that, you may be sure.'

'But Madame Hermant, she said that. . . .'

'I don't care what she said, Genista, I've told you the truth. I admit that Adrienne asked me to give the woman a job, but I had no idea that that old shrew nurtured these fantasies about us. And as for telling you. . . .' He swore softly but eloquently.

Genista turned and looked at him, her eyes wide. 'But when you were hurt at the polo match I saw her with you in the first-aid room. You were kissing her.'

'No,' he corrected her. 'She was kissing me. I was still stunned, but it didn't take me long to realise who it was and push her away. I told her then that I didn't want her.'

'You—you don't love her?' Genista asked, her voice tight in her throat.

'No. I had to wait a long time before I found the woman I really loved, the woman I wanted to spend the rest of my life with.'

Genista looked quickly away, her heart pounding so

loudly she could hear it. 'So our marriage *was* just a business arrangement, then?' she asked slowly.

'No, it wasn't. Not on my part!' he said vehemently. Then, impatiently, he swung her round to face him. 'Genista, will you please look at me? Darling, I fell in love with you from the moment you walked into my office and started yelling at me! I had to think of some way of keeping you with me. I was afraid that if I'd just let your brother go and then asked you to go out with me, you would have done so only out of gratitude. And it wasn't gratitude I wanted,' he added forcefully. 'Then, when I asked you if you were engaged, I saw you hesitate. I got pretty desperate then, and I decided to ask you to marry me to save your brother. I knew that if you had really loved someone else you would have refused, even in those circumstances.'

He looked at her searchingly, but when she didn't answer he went on urgently. 'I know it was a dirty trick. I know I deserve to be whipped for using it, but I couldn't just let you walk out of my life, not after I'd found you. I'd have done almost anything to keep you with me.'

Her eyes flickered up to him for a moment and then away again. His jaw tightened and he straightened up, leaning against the wall, deliberately looking away. 'I thought I could make you love me, Genista. I thought that once I got you on the island, once I'd shown you how much you meant to me....' he broke off. 'But you fought me off and tried to run away. God, what a mess I made of everything! I couldn't believe that you were still a virgin. And I couldn't bear to think of you holding out on me. The Greek in me really came out that night, didn't it? I wanted you so much. Everything was primitive and raw. And then you tried to kill yourself because of me.' His voice was suddenly full of pain. 'God, Genista, that really showed me what a brute I'd been. I took you away from Akasia just as fast as I could, terrified that you'd try it again. Then I had to start to undo all the harm I'd caused, try to make amends in the hope that one day you might start to care a little in return. I thought, I hoped, that I was beginning to succeed. When I kissed you that night just before you left me, and you responded, I thought for one wild and wonderful moment.... But then you pulled away and I cursed myself for every kind of a fool for letting myself get carried away again, for letting you see how much I wanted you.'

Marc turned his head at last to look at her, but Genista was staring fixedly down at her hands. 'So there you have it,' he said shortly. 'I hurt you and made you unhappy and finally drove you away, when all I wanted to do was love and cherish you. You've every right to ask for your freedom and I ought to give it to you. I know I haven't got a hope in hell of your agreeing, but I had to come and see you. I had to try.'

'Agreeing to what?' She had been still and silent for so long that he was almost surprised when she spoke.

'To come back to me. I'd agree to any terms you wanted to make,' he went on earnestly before she could speak. 'You needn't be afraid that I'd force myself on you again. I've learnt that lesson if I've learnt nothing else,' he said bitterly.

'You mean that we'd go on as we were before?' she asked slowly.

'Yes. Anything you want.'

She thought for a moment, then said decisively, 'No, I'm afraid that isn't good enough.' Her eyes bright, she turned to face him. 'Because I'm sick of this cheap imitation of a marriage! And I'm sick of lying alone in that huge bed when all the time I want to be with you, feel your arms round me, have you love me like you did before.'

She tried to go on, but Marc had seized her arms so tightly that it hurt. 'Genista, what did you say?' He was staring at her incredulously, a light of hope and wonder in his eyes.

'Oh, Marc, how can you be so blind? I've been crazy about you for ages.'

His hand came up to touch her face and Genista could feel it trembling against her skin. 'Oh, my darling, *mon ange*. We'll hire the bridal suite in the New York Hilton, we'll....'

But Genista didn't let him finish. She put a hand in his hair and drew his head down to kiss him with all the pent-up emotion she had been hiding for so long.

Above their heads a buzzer sounded unheeded, then it came again a second and third time. Eventually an irate elderly woman made her way to the galley and jerked the curtain aside. When she saw the two of them in each other's arms, completely oblivious of her presence, she said disdainfully, 'These air hostesses! They're all the same!'

But they didn't spend the night in some luxurious hotel after all, for the plane developed a fault in an engine and they were redirected to the Azores. The cabin crew were kept busy finding accommodation for all the passengers and it wasn't until late in the evening that Genista was able to get away. Marc had booked the best room he could find, but it was a long way from what he intended, as he remarked ruefully when he escorted her into it.

'Never mind, we were lucky to get it.' Genista dropped her flight bag on the dressing table and began to take off her hat.

'It's a good job you were wearing your wedding ring or they might have questioned our motives.' He came across to sit and watch her as she unpinned her hair. 'The fact that you hadn't given that back was the only hope I had,' he told her softly.

Taking her hairbrush from her bag, she said slowly, 'I was going to send it back to you, but—I couldn't.'

Marc came to stand behind her and took the brush to do it for her. She watched him in the mirror for a while, then said tentatively, 'Marc?'

'Mm?'

'It's been over two months since I left you. If—if you loved me, why didn't you come before now?'

The brush was still suddenly as his eyes met hers in the mirror. 'Because I didn't know where you were.'

'You didn't think to check with the airline?' she asked, puzzled.

'No. If you remember, you left the same night as Aly flew back to Africa. I thought you'd gone with him.' He said it quietly enough, but there was an undercurrent of remembered pain in his voice.

'Oh, Marc!' Her eyes were wide as she stared at him.

'When I opened that parcel you sent and saw the money, I was sure it was Aly. I couldn't think where else you would get such a large sum, you see. I flew after him as soon as I could get a plane, but he'd gone on somewhere else and it took me days of following him all over Africa before I finally caught up with him. I thought he was leading me on deliberately and I was almost ready to murder him when I found him. In my book a man doesn't try to steal his friend's wife, although God knows I'd given you enough cause to run away. But every time I thought of him with you, making love to you....' His mouth twisted and it was a few moments before he went on, 'When I found him I started to tear him apart, until he got in one or two punches that stopped me long enough for him to ask what the hell I was playing at. When he found out he told me a few home truths, including the fact that you'd seen me with Adrienne, that you were much too good for me and that it served me damn well right if you had left me.'

He sat down on the bed and pulled her down beside him. 'Aren't you going to take your jacket off?'

'I suppose so. What did you do then?' She slipped off her jacket and he threw it on to a chair.

'I thought that even if you hadn't run off with Aly you might have gone to him for help and that he'd hidden you away somewhere, so I started to backtrack across Africa, looking for you.'

Genista suddenly remembered the newspaper photo when he had looked so worried and unhappy and she realised a little of the agony of mind he had gone through. At least she had known where he was, that he was safe.

'I shall have to apologise to Aly,' Marc went on ruefully. 'I accused him of some terrible things.' His hand had been resting lightly on her shoulder and now he bent his head to gently bite her ear lobe, and then his lips began to explore her neck.

'Go on,' she prompted rather breathlessly.

'There's nothing much more to tell. I suddenly found out that your brother had sold his invention—to my rivals, by the way—which serves me right for having treated him so badly, and I thought you might have gone to him. I'd sent people out to trace him when my solicitors told me you'd written to them. That letter—it was quite a facer,' he said slowly. 'But at least it gave me hope that I might be able to get you back.'

For a moment his face mirrored the two months of worry and anxiety he had gone through. To try to atone she said slowly, 'Marc, that night on the island—I lied to you. I got cramp when I went swimming in the bay. You saved my life when you took me back.' She lowered her head. 'I wanted to hurt you, you see. I didn't try to kill myself at all.'

His hands came up to cup her face. 'I'm glad. You don't know how that thought tortured me.'

'I know. I'm sorry.'

'Forget it. It's behind us now.' He kissed her lingeringly and gently, taking his time. 'Don't you want to take something else off?' he asked presently.

Genista laughed and pushed him away. She stood up and began to unpack her flight bag. 'At least when we go back to France we won't have to pretend when we go to parties,' she remarked. 'It was that act you put on, so attentive and loving, that made me really hate you at first. It was so hypocritical.'

Marc lay back on the bed and watched her lazily. 'But it wasn't an act, was it? Not on my part.'

She turned and looked at him then. 'Wasn't it?'

Something in her voice made him get up quickly and come to stand close beside her, his eyes intense.

'Oh, *ma mie*, please don't look at me like that. Don't you believe it yet? That was the only time I could really be myself, show my real feelings, behave as I so much

wanted to behave towards you. I love you, *ma belle*,
my darling. I wanted the whole world to know how
much. And you, my little love, were the only one who
didn't realise it.'

For a moment she could only gaze at him as he tried
so urgently to convince her, then a new light came into
her eyes and she moved quickly into his arms. 'Oh,
Marc, it hurt so much. To fall for you and think that you
might care for me a little, and then to know that you'd
been using me all along.' Her voice was muffled in his
shoulder as he held her tightly.

His hand came up to stroke her hair and he murmured
endearments in a mixture of languages, content for the
moment to just hold her, to let her feel the warmth and
reassurance of his arms. But presently Genista lifted her
head and said on a questioning note, 'Marc, when we
went back to Akasia and you went for a swim that
night....' She paused, then went on slowly, 'You went
back to the village.'

'Yes, I thought I'd better keep away from the villa.
You were too much of a temptation. I went back to the
taverna and stayed there for the night. But how did you
know I went to the village?'

'Oh, I—I sort of waited,' she admitted, not looking at
him. 'But then I saw you and I thought you'd gone to
the girl who made eyes at you.'

He put a finger under her chin, forcing her head up,
a glint of amusement in his eyes. 'Do I detect a note of
jealousy?'

Genista tossed her head. 'Good heavens, no! What do I
care about your—your....'

'Penthouse popsies,' he supplied for her with laughter
in his voice. Then he added seriously, 'But I hope you

care, Genista. I hope you go on caring for the rest of your life. Because I swear to you that from the moment I met you I knew that there would never be another woman for me. So I'm afraid that you'll just have to put up with me, my darling, and I shall be very, very demanding.'

His lips came down to find hers in little kisses that explored her mouth, intoxicating her, making her head whirl as they became deeper and more passionate. But before she succumbed completely to his embrace, she remembered to whisper happily, 'Thank you, Aphrodite.'

Mills & Boon

Accept 4
Best Selling Romances
Absolutely
FREE

Enjoy the very best of love, romance and intrigue brought to you by Mills & Boon. Every month Mills & Boon very carefully select 4 Romances that have been particularly popular in the past and re-issue them for the benefit of readers who may have missed them first time round. Become a subscriber and you can receive all 4 superb novels every month, and your personal membership card will entitle you to a whole range of special benefits too: a free monthly newsletter, packed with exclusive book offers, recipes, competitions and your guide to the stars, plus there are other bargain offers and big cash savings.

**AND an Introductory FREE GIFT for YOU.
Turn over the page for details.**

As a special introduction we will send you
FOUR superb and exciting
Best Seller Romances – yours to keep Free
– when you complete and return
this coupon to us.

At the same time we will reserve a
subscription to Mills & Boon Best Seller
Romances for you. Every month you will
receive the 4 specially selected Best Seller
novels delivered direct to your door. Postage
and packing is always completely Free.
There is no obligation or commitment –
you can cancel your subscription
at any time.

You have absolutely nothing to lose and a whole world of
romance to gain. Simply fill in and post the coupon today to:-
MILLS & BOON READER SERVICE, FREEPOST,
P.O. BOX 236, CROYDON, SURREY CR9 9EL.

Please note:- READERS IN SOUTH AFRICA write to
Mills & Boon Ltd., Postbag X3010,
Randburg 2125, S. Africa.

- -

FREE BOOKS CERTIFICATE

**To: Mills & Boon Reader Service, FREEPOST, P.O. Box 236,
Croydon, Surrey CR9 9EL.**

Please send me, free and without obligation, four Mills & Boon Best Seller Romances, &
reserve a Reader Service Subscription for me. If I decide to subscribe I shall receive four new
books each month for £4.00, post and packing free. If I decide not to subscribe, I shall write
to you within 10 days. The free books are mine to keep in any case. I understand that I may
cancel my subscription at any time simply by writing to you. I am over 18 years of age.
Please write in BLOCK CAPITALS.

Name _____

Address _____

_____

_____ Postcode _____

SEND NO MONEY — TAKE NO RISKS.
*Remember, postcodes speed delivery. Offer applies in UK only and is not valid to
present subscribers. Mills & Boon reserve the right to exercise discretion
in granting membership. If price changes are necessary you will be noti-
fied. Offer expires 31st December 1984.*

4BS

EP10